The Last Enchanter

The Last Enchanter

Felix Northwood

Contents

1

Prologue

Setting the Scene

In the ancient land of Eldoria, magic once flowed as freely as the rivers that carved through its lush valleys. Enchanters, with their boundless power, shaped the world, bringing prosperity and peace. Cities gleamed with enchanted lights, forests whispered secrets, and the skies shimmered with the hues of countless spells. But as centuries passed, the magic began to wane. The once vibrant spells grew faint, and the Enchanters, guardians of this mystical force, dwindled in number. Eldoria, now a shadow of its former glory, teetered on the brink of darkness.

The Last Enchanter

In a secluded village, hidden from the eyes of those who sought to exploit the last remnants of magic, lived Elara. She was the final beacon of hope, the last of the Enchanters. Her mentor, Master Thalion, lay on his deathbed, his once powerful aura now a mere flicker. With a trembling hand, he reached out to Elara, his eyes filled with a mixture of sorrow and urgency.

"Elara," he whispered, his voice barely audible, "the darkness... it is returning. You must find the ancient relics... only then can you restore the magic and save Eldoria. Beware the shadows, for they seek to consume all that is left."

As his final breath left him, a chilling wind swept through the village, carrying with it the ominous promise of the trials to come. Elara, now alone, felt the weight of her destiny settle upon her shoulders. She knew that the path ahead would be fraught with danger, but she was determined to honor her mentor's dying wish and save the world she loved.

2

Chapter 1: The Awakening

Elara's Village

The village of Eldenwood nestled quietly in the heart of Eldoria, a place where time seemed to stand still. Cobblestone paths wound through clusters of quaint cottages, their thatched roofs covered in moss and ivy. The air was filled with the scent of blooming wildflowers and the distant murmur of the river that bordered the village. Eldenwood was a haven of peace, untouched by the turmoil that had begun to spread across the land.

Elara moved through the village with a grace that belied her youth. Her long, auburn hair flowed behind her like a banner, and her emerald eyes sparkled with a quiet wisdom. She was beloved by the villagers, not just for her kind heart but for the subtle magic she wielded to ease their burdens. With a mere touch, she could mend a broken tool, heal a sick child, or coax a stubborn plant to bloom.

This morning, like every other, Elara began her day at the village square. She greeted the baker, who handed her a warm loaf of bread, and the blacksmith, who nodded in appreciation as she whispered a spell to strengthen his forge. The villagers went about their routines, comforted by her presence and the small miracles she performed.

As Elara made her way to the edge of the village, she paused to admire the view. The rolling hills beyond were dotted with ancient oaks and vibrant meadows, a testament to the magic that still lingered in the land. Yet, even here, she could sense the subtle changes—the way the light seemed dimmer, the air heavier. It was as if Eldoria itself was holding its breath, waiting for something to happen.

Her thoughts were interrupted by the sound of hurried footsteps. She turned to see a group of children running towards her, their faces alight with excitement.

"Elara! Elara!" they called out, their voices a chorus of joy. "Come see what we found!"

She smiled and followed them to a small clearing near the river. There, nestled among the reeds, was a nest of baby birds, their tiny beaks open wide in hunger. Elara knelt down, her heart swelling with tenderness. She whispered a soft incantation, and the reeds around the nest began to shimmer with a gentle, golden light. The birds chirped happily as they were enveloped in the warmth of her magic.

"Thank you, Elara," one of the children said, his eyes wide with wonder. "You're amazing."

She ruffled his hair affectionately. "It's nothing, really. Just a little magic."

As the children scampered off, Elara stood and gazed out at the river. A sense of unease settled over her. The strange occurrences she had noticed lately—the sudden changes in weather, the animals acting out of character—were becoming more frequent. She couldn't shake the feeling that something was coming, something that would change their world forever.

With a sigh, she turned back towards the village. She had responsibilities here, people who depended on her. But in the back of her mind, the words of her mentor echoed like a distant thunderclap: "Beware the shadows, for they seek to consume all that is left."

Elara knew that her peaceful life in Eldenwood was about to be disrupted. The awakening had begun, and she would need to be ready for whatever lay ahead.

The Omen

The sun hung low in the sky, casting long shadows across Eldenwood as Elara made her way back to the village. The air was unusually still, and a sense of foreboding settled over her like a heavy cloak. She couldn't shake the feeling that something was amiss.

As she approached the village square, she noticed a group of villagers gathered around the well, their faces etched with worry. Elara quickened her pace, her heart pounding in her chest.

"What's happened?" she asked, pushing her way through the crowd.

"It's the animals, Elara," said Old Man Harlen, his voice trembling. "They're acting strange. The cows won't give milk, and the chickens are refusing to lay eggs. Even the dogs are restless, barking at shadows."

Elara frowned, her mind racing. She had sensed the disturbances, but this was more than she had anticipated. She knelt beside the well and placed her hand on the cool stone, closing her eyes to focus her magic. A faint, dark energy pulsed beneath her fingertips, sending a shiver down her spine.

"It's not just the animals," she said, opening her eyes. "There's something else at work here. Something dark."

The villagers exchanged uneasy glances, their fear palpable. Elara stood and faced them, her expression resolute.

"I'll look into it," she promised. "But for now, try to stay calm and keep an eye on each other. We'll get through this."

As the crowd began to disperse, Elara felt a tug on her sleeve. She turned to see a young girl, no more than six years old, clutching a ragged doll to her chest.

"Elara," the girl whispered, her eyes wide with fear. "I saw a shadow in my room last night. It was big and scary."

Elara knelt down to the girl's level, her heart aching at the sight of her fear. "It's okay, little one," she said softly. "I'll make sure the shadows stay away."

The girl nodded, her grip on the doll tightening. Elara watched as she ran back to her mother, who gave Elara a grateful smile before leading her daughter home.

As the last of the villagers returned to their homes, Elara stood alone in the square, the weight of their fears pressing down on her. She knew she had to act quickly. The disturbances were growing stronger, and she couldn't afford to wait any longer.

She made her way to the edge of the village, where the forest loomed dark and foreboding. The trees whispered secrets in the fading light, their branches swaying in an unseen breeze. Elara took a deep breath and stepped into the shadows, her senses on high alert.

The forest was eerily silent, the usual sounds of wildlife absent. Elara moved cautiously, her eyes scanning the darkness for any sign of danger. As she ventured deeper, she felt the dark energy growing stronger, pulling her towards its source.

Suddenly, a rustling sound broke the silence. Elara spun around, her hand instinctively reaching for the small dagger at her waist. A pair of glowing eyes stared back at her from the underbrush, and a low growl rumbled through the air.

"Who's there?" Elara called out, her voice steady despite the fear gnawing at her insides.

The creature stepped into the light, revealing itself to be a large, black wolf. Its fur bristled, and its eyes glowed with an unnatural light. Elara held her ground, her magic thrumming just beneath the surface.

"Easy now," she said softly, extending her hand. "I'm not here to hurt you."

The wolf hesitated, its growl fading to a low whine. Elara took a step forward, her magic reaching out to soothe the creature. The wolf's eyes softened, and it lowered its head, allowing her to approach.

Elara knelt beside the wolf, her hand gently stroking its fur. "What happened to you?" she murmured, sensing the dark energy that clung to the creature. "Who did this?"

The wolf let out a soft whimper, and Elara felt a surge of anger. Whatever was causing the disturbances in Eldenwood was powerful, and it was growing stronger by the day. She knew she had to find the source and put an end to it before it consumed everything she held dear.

With a final pat, Elara stood and watched as the wolf disappeared into the shadows. She turned back towards the village, her resolve hardening. The awakening had begun, and she would need all her strength and courage to face the darkness that threatened to engulf Eldoria.

The Council's Summons

The next morning, Elara awoke with a sense of unease that had settled deep in her bones. The events of the previous day weighed heavily on her mind. She knew she had to find answers, but she didn't expect them to come so soon.

As she prepared for the day, a sudden flash of light filled her small cottage. Startled, she turned to see a glowing orb hovering in the center of the room. It pulsed with a soft, golden light, and Elara recognized it immediately—a summons from the magical council.

She reached out and touched the orb, feeling a warm, tingling sensation spread through her fingers. The orb expanded, and a voice echoed in her mind, clear and urgent.

"Elara, last of the Enchanters, you are summoned to the Council of Eldoria. The time has come for you to fulfill your destiny. Make haste, for the darkness grows stronger with each passing day."

The orb vanished as quickly as it had appeared, leaving Elara standing in stunned silence. The council had been silent for years, their numbers dwindling as the magic faded. For them to reach out now meant that the situation was dire.

Determined, Elara gathered her belongings. She packed a small satchel with essentials—her spellbook, a few potions, and the dagger her mentor had given her. She donned her cloak, its deep green fabric blending seamlessly with the forest, and stepped out into the crisp morning air.

The villagers were already awake, going about their daily routines. As Elara made her way through the village, she was met with curious glances and concerned whispers. Word of the strange occurrences had spread quickly, and the villagers looked to her for reassurance.

"Elara, where are you going?" called out Maren, the village healer, her brow furrowed with worry.

"I've been summoned by the council," Elara replied, her voice steady. "I need to find out what's causing these disturbances and put an end to it."

Maren nodded, her expression softening. "Be careful, Elara. We'll be waiting for your return."

Elara smiled and continued on her way, her heart heavy with the weight of their expectations. She knew the journey ahead would be perilous, but she couldn't let them down.

As she reached the edge of the village, she paused to take one last look at the place she had called home. The sun was just beginning to rise, casting a golden glow over the rooftops. She took a deep breath, steeling herself for the challenges ahead, and stepped onto the path that led into the forest.

The journey to the council's meeting place was long and arduous. Elara traveled through dense forests, across rocky terrain, and over rushing rivers. The landscape of Eldoria was beautiful, but it was also a stark reminder of the magic that was slipping away. The trees no longer whispered secrets, and the air was thick with an oppressive silence.

As she traveled, Elara encountered various creatures—some friendly, others not. She used her magic sparingly, conserving her strength for the trials she knew awaited her. Each night, she camped under the stars, her thoughts drifting to her mentor's final words and the prophecy that had been revealed to her.

After several days of travel, Elara finally reached her destination. Hidden deep within the heart of the forest was an ancient sanctuary, its entrance marked by towering stone pillars covered in intricate runes. The air here was thick with magic, a stark contrast to the fading energy she had felt elsewhere.

Elara stepped through the entrance, her footsteps echoing in the silence. The sanctuary was a vast, open space, its walls lined with shelves of ancient tomes and artifacts. At the center of the room stood a circular table, around which sat the remaining members of the magical council.

The council members were a diverse group, each representing a different aspect of Eldoria's magical heritage. There was Thalindra, the wise and aged elf; Borin, the stout and sturdy dwarf; and Seraphina, the ethereal and enigmatic fae. They looked up as Elara approached, their expressions a mix of relief and concern.

"Elara," Thalindra said, her voice soft but commanding. "We are glad you have come. The darkness we feared is upon us, and only you can stop it."

Elara nodded, her resolve hardening. "Tell me what I must do."

The council members exchanged glances before Thalindra spoke again. "There is a prophecy, one that speaks of the Last Enchanter who will save Eldoria. You must find the ancient relics, hidden throughout the land. Only with their combined power can you restore the magic and defeat the darkness."

Elara listened intently, her mind racing with the enormity of the task ahead. She knew it would not be easy, but she was ready to face whatever challenges lay in her path.

With the council's guidance and the weight of destiny on her shoulders, Elara set out on her quest, determined to save Eldoria and fulfill her mentor's dying wish.

The Journey Begins

Elara stepped out of the sanctuary, the weight of the council's words heavy on her mind. The path ahead was uncertain, but she knew she had to press on. The forest around her was dense and dark, the trees towering above like silent sentinels. She adjusted her cloak and tightened her grip on her staff, ready to face whatever lay ahead.

The journey was arduous, the terrain unforgiving. Elara moved with purpose, her senses heightened by the lingering magic in the air. The forest was alive with the sounds of rustling leaves and distant animal calls, but there was an underlying tension that set her on edge. She couldn't shake the feeling that she was being watched.

As she traveled deeper into the forest, the landscape began to change. The trees grew thicker, their branches intertwining to form a canopy that blocked out the sun. The air grew cooler, and a faint mist clung to the ground. Elara's footsteps were muffled by the soft, moss-covered earth.

She paused to take a sip from her water flask, her eyes scanning the surroundings. The forest seemed to close in around her, the shadows deepening with each step. She took a deep breath, centering herself, and continued on.

Hours passed, and the forest showed no signs of thinning. Elara's muscles ached from the constant walking, but she pushed on, driven by the urgency of her mission. As she rounded a bend in the path, she spotted a small clearing up ahead. Relieved, she quickened her pace.

The clearing was a welcome respite from the oppressive forest. Sunlight filtered through the trees, casting dappled patterns on the ground. In the center of the clearing stood a large, ancient oak tree, its gnarled branches reaching towards the sky. Elara approached the tree, sensing a faint magical energy emanating from it.

She placed her hand on the rough bark, closing her eyes to focus her magic. The tree responded, its energy mingling with hers. Images flashed through her mind—visions of the past, of Enchanters who had come before her, and of the dark forces that now threatened Eldoria. The tree's magic was ancient and powerful, a remnant of a time when magic was abundant.

As Elara delved deeper into the tree's memories, she felt a sudden jolt of energy. Her eyes snapped open, and she stumbled back, her heart racing. The tree had shown her a vision of a hidden path, one that would lead her to the first of the ancient relics.

Determined, Elara set off in the direction the tree had indicated. The path was narrow and overgrown, barely visible beneath the underbrush. She pushed through the foliage, her staff cutting a swath through the dense vegetation.

The journey was slow and treacherous, the path winding through rocky terrain and across shallow streams. Elara's senses were on high alert, every rustle of leaves and snap of twigs putting her on edge. She knew she was not alone in the forest.

As she climbed a steep hill, she heard a low growl behind her. She spun around, her staff at the ready, and came face to face with a large, black bear. The bear's eyes glowed with an unnatural light, and its fur bristled with dark energy.

Elara took a step back, her heart pounding. She could feel the dark magic emanating from the creature, a twisted force that sought to consume everything in its path. She knew she had to act quickly.

Raising her staff, Elara chanted a spell, her voice steady and clear. A beam of light shot from the staff, striking the bear and enveloping it in a shimmering aura. The bear roared in pain, its dark energy dissipating as the light purified it.

With a final, agonized growl, the bear collapsed to the ground, its eyes returning to their natural, dark brown color. Elara approached cautiously, her staff still glowing with residual magic. She knelt beside the bear, her hand gently resting on its fur.

"I'm sorry," she whispered, her voice filled with sorrow. "I had no choice."

The bear let out a soft whimper before closing its eyes, its breathing slow and steady. Elara stood, her heart heavy with the weight of what she had done. She knew the darkness was spreading, corrupting the creatures of the forest, and she had to stop it.

With renewed determination, Elara continued on her journey, the path ahead clearer than ever. She knew the challenges would only grow more difficult, but she was ready to face them. The fate of Eldoria depended on her, and she would not let her people down.

The Prophecy

Elara emerged from the dense forest, her body weary but her spirit unbroken. Before her lay the ancient sanctuary, its stone walls covered in moss and ivy, a testament to its age and the magic it held within. The entrance was marked by towering pillars, each inscribed with runes that glowed faintly in the dim light. She took a deep breath, feeling the weight of her journey lift slightly as she stepped into the hallowed ground.

The sanctuary was a vast, open space, its high ceilings supported by intricately carved columns. Shelves lined the walls, filled with ancient tomes and artifacts that hummed with residual magic. At the center of the room stood a circular table, around which sat the remaining members of the magical council. Their faces were etched with lines of worry and fatigue, but their eyes held a glimmer of hope as they looked upon Elara.

"Welcome, Elara," Thalindra, the eldest of the council, greeted her with a nod. Her silver hair flowed like a river down her back, and her eyes, though weary, sparkled with wisdom. "We have been expecting you."

Elara bowed respectfully. "Thank you, Thalindra. I came as soon as I received your summons."

Borin, the stout dwarf with a beard as thick as a forest, grunted in approval. "Aye, and not a moment too soon. The darkness is spreading faster than we anticipated."

Seraphina, the ethereal fae with wings that shimmered like moonlight, floated gracefully to Elara's side. "You have done well to come this far, Elara. But the journey ahead will be even more perilous."

Elara nodded, her resolve hardening. "I am ready. Tell me what I must do."

Thalindra gestured to a large, ancient tome that lay open on the table. The pages were filled with intricate illustrations and flowing script, detailing the history of Eldoria and the prophecy that had been passed down through generations.

"The prophecy speaks of the Last Enchanter," Thalindra began, her voice echoing softly in the chamber. "It is said that only the Last Enchanter can restore the magic to Eldoria and defeat the darkness that threatens to consume it. To do this, you must find the ancient relics, hidden through-out the land. Each relic holds a piece of the magic that once flowed freely through Eldoria."

Elara listened intently, her mind racing with the enormity of the task ahead. "Where do I begin?"

Borin stepped forward, his expression serious. "The first relic is the Amulet of Light, hidden in the ruins of the Lost City. It is said to be guarded by powerful enchantments and creatures of the dark. You must retrieve it and bring it back here."

Seraphina placed a gentle hand on Elara's shoulder. "You will not be alone in this quest. We will provide you with what aid we can, but the journey is yours to undertake."

Elara took a deep breath, feeling the weight of her destiny settle upon her shoulders. "I understand. I will find the Amulet of Light and bring it back."

Thalindra smiled, a glimmer of pride in her eyes. "We have faith in you, Elara. You are the last hope for Eldoria."

With the council's guidance and the prophecy clear in her mind, Elara set out from the sanctuary, her heart filled with determination. The path ahead was fraught with danger, but she knew she had to succeed. The fate of Eldoria depended on her, and she would not let her people down.

As she stepped back into the forest, the shadows seemed to part before her, as if acknowledging her resolve. Elara tightened her grip on her staff and began her journey towards the Lost City, ready to face whatever challenges lay in her path. The awakening had begun, and she was determined to see it through to the end.

Chapter 2: The Call to Adventure

The Council's Summons

Elara awoke to the soft glow of dawn filtering through the small window of her cottage. The events of the previous days weighed heavily on her mind, but she felt a renewed sense of purpose. She knew her journey was just beginning. As she stretched and prepared for the day, a sudden flash of light filled the room, startling her.

Hovering in the center of the room was a small, glowing orb, pulsating with a soft, golden light. Elara recognized it immediately—a summons from the magical council. Her heart quickened as she reached out to touch the orb. The moment her fingers brushed its surface, a warm, tingling sensation spread through her hand, and a voice echoed in her mind.

"Elara, last of the Enchanters, you are summoned to the Council of Eldoria. The time has come for you to fulfill your destiny. Make haste, for the darkness grows stronger with each passing day."

The orb vanished as quickly as it had appeared, leaving Elara standing in stunned silence. The council had been silent for years, their numbers dwindling as the magic faded. For them to reach out now meant that the situation was dire.

Determined, Elara began to gather her belongings. She packed a small satchel with essentials—her spellbook, a few potions, and the dagger her mentor had given her. She donned her cloak, its deep green fabric blending seamlessly with the forest, and stepped out into the crisp morning air.

The village of Eldenwood was already stirring. Villagers went about their morning routines, but there was an undercurrent of unease. Word of the strange occurrences had spread quickly, and the villagers looked to Elara for reassurance.

As she made her way through the village, she was met with curious glances and concerned whispers. Maren, the village healer, approached her with a worried expression.

"Elara, where are you going?" Maren asked, her brow furrowed.

"I've been summoned by the council," Elara replied, her voice steady. "I need to find out what's causing these disturbances and put an end to it."

Maren nodded, her expression softening. "Be careful, Elara. We'll be waiting for your return."

Elara smiled and continued on her way, her heart heavy with the weight of their expectations. She knew the journey ahead would be perilous, but she couldn't let them down.

As she reached the edge of the village, she paused to take one last look at the place she had called home. The sun was just beginning to rise, casting a golden glow over the rooftops. She took a deep breath, steeling herself for the challenges ahead, and stepped onto the path that led into the forest.

The journey to the council's meeting place was long and arduous. Elara traveled through dense forests, across rocky terrain, and over rushing rivers. The landscape of Eldoria was beautiful, but it was also a stark reminder of the magic that was slipping away. The trees no longer whispered secrets, and the air was thick with an oppressive silence.

As she traveled, Elara encountered various creatures—some friendly, others not. She used her magic sparingly, conserving her strength for the trials she knew awaited her. Each night, she camped under the stars, her thoughts drifting to her mentor's final words and the prophecy that had been revealed to her.

After several days of travel, Elara finally reached her destination. Hidden deep within the heart of the forest was an ancient sanctuary, its entrance marked by towering stone pillars covered in intricate runes. The air here was thick with magic, a stark contrast to the fading energy she had felt elsewhere.

Elara stepped through the entrance, her footsteps echoing in the silence. The sanctuary was a vast, open space, its walls lined with shelves of ancient tomes and artifacts. At the center of the room stood a circular table, around which sat the remaining members of the magical council.

The council members were a diverse group, each representing a different aspect of Eldoria's magical heritage. There was Thalindra, the wise and aged elf; Borin, the stout and sturdy dwarf; and Seraphina, the ethereal and enigmatic fae. They looked up as Elara approached, their expressions a mix of relief and concern.

"Elara," Thalindra said, her voice soft but commanding. "We are glad you have come. The darkness we feared is upon us, and only you can stop it."

Elara nodded, her resolve hardening. "Tell me what I must do."

The council members exchanged glances before Thalindra spoke again. "There is a prophecy, one that speaks of the Last Enchanter who will save Eldoria. You must find the ancient relics, hidden throughout the land. Only with their combined power can you restore the magic and defeat the darkness."

Elara listened intently, her mind racing with the enormity of the task ahead. She knew it would not be easy, but she was ready to face whatever challenges lay in her path.

With the council's guidance and the weight of destiny on her shoulders, Elara set out from the sanctuary, determined to save Eldoria and fulfill her mentor's dying wish.

The Journey Begins

Elara stepped out of the sanctuary, the weight of the council's words heavy on her mind. The path ahead was uncertain, but she knew she had to press on. The forest around her was dense and dark, the trees towering above like silent sentinels. She adjusted her cloak and tightened her grip on her staff, ready to face whatever lay ahead.

The journey was arduous, the terrain unforgiving. Elara moved with purpose, her senses heightened by the lingering magic in the air. The forest was alive with the sounds of rustling leaves and distant animal calls, but there was an underlying tension that set her on edge. She couldn't shake the feeling that she was being watched.

As she traveled deeper into the forest, the landscape began to change. The trees grew thicker, their branches intertwining to form a canopy that blocked out the sun. The air grew cooler, and a faint mist clung to the ground. Elara's footsteps were muffled by the soft, moss-covered earth.

She paused to take a sip from her water flask, her eyes scanning the surroundings. The forest seemed to close in around her, the shadows deepening with each step. She took a deep breath, centering herself, and continued on.

Hours passed, and the forest showed no signs of thinning. Elara's muscles ached from the constant walking, but she pushed on, driven by the urgency of her mission. As she rounded a bend in the path, she spotted a small clearing up ahead. Relieved, she quickened her pace.

The clearing was a welcome respite from the oppressive forest. Sunlight filtered through the trees, casting dappled patterns on the ground. In the center of the clearing stood a large, ancient oak tree, its gnarled branches reaching towards the sky. Elara approached the tree, sensing a faint magical energy emanating from it.

She placed her hand on the rough bark, closing her eyes to focus her magic. The tree responded, its energy mingling with hers. Images flashed through her mind—visions of the past, of Enchanters who had come before her, and of the dark forces that now threatened Eldoria. The tree's magic was ancient and powerful, a remnant of a time when magic was abundant.

As Elara delved deeper into the tree's memories, she felt a sudden jolt of energy. Her eyes snapped open, and she stumbled back, her heart racing. The tree had shown her a vision of a hidden path, one that would lead her to the first of the ancient relics.

Determined, Elara set off in the direction the tree had indicated. The path was narrow and overgrown, barely visible beneath the underbrush. She pushed through the foliage, her staff cutting a swath through the dense vegetation.

The journey was slow and treacherous, the path winding through rocky terrain and across shallow streams. Elara's senses were on high alert, every rustle of leaves and snap of twigs putting her on edge. She knew she was not alone in the forest.

As she climbed a steep hill, she heard a low growl behind her. She spun around, her staff at the ready, and came face to face with a large, black bear. The bear's eyes glowed with an unnatural light, and its fur bristled with dark energy.

Elara took a step back, her heart pounding. She could feel the dark magic emanating from the creature, a twisted force that sought to consume everything in its path. She knew she had to act quickly.

Raising her staff, Elara chanted a spell, her voice steady and clear. A beam of light shot from the staff, striking the bear and enveloping it in a shimmering aura. The bear

roared in pain, its dark energy dissipating as the light purified it.

With a final, agonized growl, the bear collapsed to the
ground, its eyes returning to their natural, dark brown
color. Elara approached cautiously, her staff still glowing
with residual magic. She knelt beside the bear, her hand
gently resting on its fur.

"I'm sorry," she whispered, her voice filled with sorrow.
"I had no choice."

The bear let out a soft whimper before closing its eyes,
its breathing slow and steady. Elara stood, her heart heavy
with the weight of what she had done. She knew the darkness was spreading, corrupting the creatures of the forest,
and she had to stop it.

With renewed determination, Elara continued on her
journey, the path ahead clearer than ever. She knew the
challenges would only grow more difficult, but she was
ready to face them. The fate of Eldoria depended on her, and
she would not let her people down.

The First Companion

Elara continued her journey through the dense forest,
the path winding and treacherous. The sun was beginning
to set, casting long shadows that danced eerily among the
trees. She knew she needed to find a safe place to camp for
the night, but the forest offered little in the way of comfort
or security.

As she rounded a bend, she spotted a small clearing up
ahead. Relieved, she quickened her pace, eager to rest her

weary legs. The clearing was bathed in the soft glow of twi-
light, and a small stream trickled nearby, its gentle murmur
soothing her frayed nerves.

Elara set down her pack and began to gather wood for a
fire. As she worked, she couldn't shake the feeling that she
was being watched. She paused, listening intently, but heard
nothing unusual. Shaking off her unease, she continued her
task, determined to have a warm fire to ward off the chill of
the night.

Just as she was about to strike a spark, a rustling sound
came from the edge of the clearing. Elara's hand went to her
staff, her senses on high alert. From the shadows emerged a
tall figure, cloaked in dark leather armor, a sword strapped
to his back. His eyes, sharp and calculating, locked onto hers.

"Who are you?" Elara demanded, her voice steady despite
the rapid beating of her heart.

The stranger raised his hands in a gesture of peace. "Easy
there. My name is Kael. I'm just passing through."

Elara narrowed her eyes, not lowering her staff. "Passing
through? In the middle of this forest?"

Kael shrugged, a hint of a smile playing at the corners
of his mouth. "I could ask you the same thing. But it seems
we're both here for a reason."

Elara studied him for a moment, sensing no immediate
threat. She lowered her staff slightly but kept her guard up.
"I'm Elara. What brings you to this part of Eldoria?"

Kael's expression grew serious. "I've been tracking the
disturbances in the land. Dark magic is spreading, and I in-
tend to find the source."

Elara's eyes widened in surprise. "You're hunting the darkness too?"

Kael nodded. "It seems our paths are aligned. Perhaps we can help each other."

Elara hesitated, her mind racing. She had been prepared to face this journey alone, but having an ally could be beneficial. Still, she couldn't afford to trust him completely just yet.

"Why should I trust you?" she asked, her voice firm.

Kael's gaze softened. "Because we both want the same thing—to save Eldoria. And because it's dangerous to travel alone."

Elara considered his words, weighing her options. Finally, she nodded. "Alright. We can travel together. But know this—if you betray me, you'll regret it."

Kael chuckled, a genuine smile breaking through his serious demeanor. "Understood. Now, let's get that fire going. It's going to be a long night."

Together, they built a fire, its warm glow casting flickering shadows around the clearing. As they sat by the fire, Elara couldn't help but feel a sense of relief. For the first time since she had left her village, she didn't feel completely alone.

They shared stories of their pasts, each revealing bits and pieces of their lives. Kael spoke of his time as a warrior, fighting to protect his homeland from invaders. Elara told him about her village and her mentor, and the prophecy that had set her on this path.

As the night wore on, they grew more comfortable in each other's presence. Elara found herself trusting Kael more than she had expected. There was a strength and determination in him that mirrored her own, and she knew they would make a formidable team.

When the fire had burned down to embers, they settled in for the night, each taking turns to keep watch. As Elara lay beneath the stars, she felt a renewed sense of hope. The journey ahead would be difficult, but with Kael by her side, she felt ready to face whatever challenges lay in their path.

The call to adventure had brought them together, and together, they would fight to save Eldoria from the encroaching darkness.

The Hidden Library

The sun was high in the sky as Elara and Kael continued their journey through the forest. The dense canopy above provided a cool respite from the heat, but the path was becoming increasingly difficult to navigate. Vines and underbrush tangled around their feet, and the air was thick with the scent of damp earth and decaying leaves.

"We should be close," Elara said, consulting the map she had drawn from the tree's vision. "The hidden library should be just beyond this ridge."

Kael nodded, his eyes scanning the surroundings for any signs of danger. "Let's hope it's worth the trouble. We need all the information we can get."

They climbed the ridge, their progress slow but steady. As they reached the top, they were greeted by a breathtaking sight. Nestled in a secluded valley below was a grand structure, its stone walls covered in ivy and moss. The hidden library, long forgotten by most of Eldoria, stood as a testament to the ancient magic that once thrived in the land.

Elara and Kael made their way down the ridge, their excitement growing with each step. The entrance to the library was marked by a pair of massive wooden doors, intricately carved with symbols and runes. Elara placed her hand on the door, feeling the faint hum of magic that still lingered.

With a gentle push, the doors creaked open, revealing a vast hall filled with rows upon rows of ancient tomes and scrolls. The air was thick with the scent of old parchment and dust, and the only sound was the soft rustle of pages as a faint breeze stirred the room.

"This place is incredible," Kael whispered, his voice filled with awe. "I've never seen so many books in one place."

Elara nodded, her eyes wide with wonder. "This library holds the knowledge of generations of Enchanters. If there's any information about the prophecy and the relics, it will be here."

They split up, each taking a different section of the library. Elara moved through the aisles, her fingers trailing along the spines of the books. She pulled out a few volumes that looked promising, their titles hinting at ancient prophecies and forgotten magic.

Kael, meanwhile, focused on the scrolls and manuscripts. He unrolled one particularly old scroll, its delicate parchment covered in faded ink. As he read, his eyes widened in realization.

"Elara, come look at this," he called out, his voice echoing in the vast hall.

Elara hurried over, her curiosity piqued. Kael handed her the scroll, and she quickly scanned its contents. It detailed the prophecy of the Last Enchanter, describing the ancient relics and their significance in restoring the magic to Eldoria.

"This is it," Elara said, her voice trembling with excitement. "This scroll confirms everything the council told us. The relics are real, and they hold the key to saving Eldoria."

Kael nodded, his expression serious. "But it also mentions a dark mage, one who seeks to control the relics for his own gain. We need to be careful."

Elara's heart sank at the mention of the dark mage. She had sensed his presence in the forest, but seeing it written in the ancient scroll made the threat all too real. "We need to find the relics before he does. If he gets his hands on them, it could mean the end of Eldoria."

They continued their search, uncovering more information about the relics and their locations. Each piece of the puzzle brought them closer to understanding the full extent of the prophecy and the challenges they would face.

As the sun began to set, casting long shadows across the library, Elara and Kael gathered their findings and prepared to leave. They had learned much, but there was still so much to do.

"We should rest for the night," Kael suggested, his voice weary. "We'll need our strength for the journey ahead."

Elara nodded in agreement. "You're right. Let's set up camp outside. We can review our findings and plan our next move."

They exited the library, the doors closing behind them with a soft thud. The night air was cool and refreshing, a welcome change from the musty confines of the library. They set up camp near the entrance, the flickering fire casting a warm glow on their faces.

As they sat by the fire, Elara couldn't help but feel a sense of hope. They had made significant progress, and with Kael by her side, she felt more confident than ever in their ability to succeed.

"We're on the right path," she said, her voice filled with determination. "We'll find the relics and stop the dark mage. Eldoria will be saved."

Kael smiled, his eyes reflecting the firelight. "I believe in us, Elara. Together, we can do this."

With their resolve strengthened and their spirits high, they settled in for the night, ready to face whatever challenges lay ahead. The call to adventure had brought them together, and together, they would fight to save Eldoria from the encroaching darkness.

The Prophecy Unfolds

The fire crackled softly as Elara and Kael sat in the warm glow, their faces illuminated by the dancing flames. The night was quiet, the forest around them still and serene. They had spent hours poring over the ancient texts and scrolls they had found in the hidden library, piecing together the fragments of the prophecy.

Elara held the scroll that detailed the prophecy of the Last Enchanter, her eyes scanning the faded ink. "The prophecy speaks of five ancient relics," she said, her voice thoughtful. "Each one holds a piece of the magic that once flowed through Eldoria. Together, they can restore the balance and drive back the darkness."

Kael nodded, his expression serious. "We know the first relic is the Amulet of Light, hidden in the ruins of the Lost City. But what about the others?"

Elara unrolled another scroll, revealing a map of Eldoria marked with symbols and runes. "According to this map, the other relics are scattered across the land. The Sword of Dawn, the Shield of Eternity, the Crown of Stars, and the Staff of Wisdom. Each one is guarded by powerful enchantments and creatures of the dark."

Kael leaned closer, studying the map. "It won't be easy to find them. The dark mage will be searching for them too. We need to move quickly."

Elara nodded, her resolve hardening. "We can't let him get his hands on the relics. If he does, it could mean the end of Eldoria."

They sat in silence for a moment, the weight of their mission settling over them. Elara could feel the enormity of the task ahead, but she also felt a renewed sense of purpose. She had Kael by her side, and together, they would face whatever challenges lay in their path.

"We should start with the Amulet of Light," Kael said, breaking the silence. "It's the closest, and it will give us a head start on the dark mage."

Elara agreed. "The Lost City is a few days' journey from here. We'll need to be prepared for anything."

They spent the next few hours planning their route and gathering their supplies. Elara used her magic to create protective charms and potions, while Kael sharpened his sword and checked their provisions. They worked in companionable silence, each focused on their tasks.

As the night wore on, Elara felt a sense of camaraderie growing between them. Kael was a skilled warrior, but he was also kind and thoughtful. She was grateful for his presence, knowing that she couldn't do this alone.

When their preparations were complete, they settled down to rest, taking turns to keep watch. Elara lay beneath the stars, her mind racing with thoughts of the prophecy and the journey ahead. She knew the path would be fraught with danger, but she was ready to face it.

In the quiet of the night, Elara felt a sense of peace. The prophecy had brought her and Kael together, and together, they would fight to save Eldoria. She closed her eyes, letting the sounds of the forest lull her to sleep, her heart filled with hope and determination.

The dawn broke with a soft, golden light, casting a warm glow over the forest. Elara and Kael packed up their camp and set off towards the Lost City, their spirits high. The call to adventure had brought them together, and together, they would face whatever challenges lay ahead.

As they walked, Elara couldn't help but feel a sense of excitement. The prophecy was unfolding before her eyes, and she was determined to see it through to the end. With Kael by her side, she knew they could overcome any obstacle.

The journey ahead would be long and difficult, but Elara was ready. The fate of Eldoria rested in their hands, and she would not let her people down. The call to adventure had been answered, and the prophecy was in motion. Together, they would save Eldoria from the encroaching darkness.

4

Chapter 3: Gathering Allies

The Journey Begins

Elara and Kael left the hidden library at dawn, the first light of day casting long shadows across the forest floor. The air was crisp and cool, filled with the scent of pine and earth. They moved with purpose, their steps quick and sure as they followed the path towards the Lost City.

The journey was quiet at first, each of them lost in their thoughts. Elara's mind raced with the information they had uncovered in the library. The prophecy, the relics, the dark mage—it all seemed overwhelming. But she knew they had to press on. The fate of Eldoria depended on them.

As they traveled, the forest began to thin, giving way to rolling hills and open meadows. The sun climbed higher in the sky, warming their backs and lifting their spirits. They had been walking for several hours when they heard the distant sounds of shouting and clashing metal.

Kael's hand went to his sword, his eyes narrowing. "Sounds like trouble up ahead."

Elara nodded, her grip tightening on her staff. "Let's go."

They quickened their pace, the sounds growing louder as they approached a small village nestled in a valley. Smoke rose from several of the cottages, and dark creatures swarmed through the streets, attacking anyone in their path. Villagers screamed and ran, trying to fend off the attackers with whatever they could find.

Elara and Kael sprang into action. Kael drew his sword and charged into the fray, his blade flashing in the sunlight as he cut down the dark creatures. Elara raised her staff, chanting a spell that sent a wave of light through the village, driving back the attackers.

In the midst of the chaos, Elara spotted a figure darting through the shadows, moving with incredible speed and agility. It was a young woman, her dark hair tied back in a loose braid, her eyes sharp and focused. She wielded a pair of daggers with deadly precision, taking down the creatures with swift, calculated strikes.

Elara made her way towards the woman, her magic clearing a path through the attackers. "Who are you?" she called out, her voice barely audible over the din of battle.

The woman glanced at her, a wry smile on her lips. "Name's Lyra. And you?"

"Elara," she replied, sending a bolt of energy at a creature that lunged towards them. "We're here to help."

Lyra nodded, her movements never slowing. "Good. We could use it."

Together, they fought their way through the village, their combined efforts turning the tide of the battle. Kael joined them, his sword flashing as he cut down the last of the dark creatures. The village fell silent, the only sounds the crackling of the fires and the labored breathing of the survivors.

Elara turned to Lyra, her eyes filled with gratitude. "Thank you for your help. We couldn't have done it without you."

Lyra shrugged, wiping her daggers on her tunic. "I was just doing what needed to be done. These creatures have been attacking villages all over Eldoria. Someone has to stop them."

Kael sheathed his sword, his expression serious. "We're on a quest to find the ancient relics and stop the dark mage behind these attacks. We could use someone with your skills."

Lyra raised an eyebrow, her interest piqued. "Ancient relics, huh? Sounds like quite the adventure."

Elara nodded. "It is. And we could use all the help we can get. Will you join us?"

Lyra considered for a moment, her eyes scanning the village. The villagers were beginning to emerge from their homes, their faces filled with relief and gratitude. She turned back to Elara and Kael, a determined look in her eyes.

"Alright," she said, sheathing her daggers. "I'm in. Let's go find those relics and save Eldoria."

With their new ally by their side, Elara and Kael felt a renewed sense of hope. They had faced their first challenge together and emerged victorious. The journey ahead would be long and difficult, but they were no longer alone. Together, they would gather the allies they needed and fight to save their world from the encroaching darkness.

The Wise Sage

The trio set off from the village at first light, the morning sun casting a golden hue over the landscape. Elara, Kael, and their new companion Lyra moved swiftly through the forest, their steps light and purposeful. The air was filled with the sounds of birdsong and rustling leaves, a stark contrast to the chaos they had left behind.

Elara led the way, her eyes scanning the map she had drawn from the hidden library. "According to this, we should find an ancient grove not far from here. It's said to be the home of a wise sage who might have more information about the relics."

Lyra, ever the skeptic, raised an eyebrow. "A wise sage in a hidden grove? Sounds like something out of a fairy tale."

Kael chuckled, his hand resting on the hilt of his sword. "In Eldoria, fairy tales often hold more truth than you'd think."

They continued their journey, the forest growing denser with each step. The trees towered above them, their branches intertwining to form a canopy that blocked out the sun. The air grew cooler, and a faint mist clung to the ground, giving the forest an otherworldly feel.

After several hours of walking, they came upon a clearing. In the center stood a massive oak tree, its gnarled branches reaching towards the sky. The tree radiated a powerful, ancient magic, and Elara knew they had found the grove.

"Stay close," she whispered, her voice barely audible. "The sage is said to be very old and very powerful. We must show respect."

They approached the tree cautiously, their eyes scanning the surroundings for any sign of the sage. As they drew closer, a figure emerged from the shadows, his form blending seamlessly with the forest. He was an elderly man, his long white beard flowing down to his chest, his eyes sharp and piercing.

"Who dares enter my grove?" the sage demanded, his voice resonating with authority.

Elara stepped forward, her head bowed in respect. "We seek your wisdom, Eldrin. We are on a quest to find the ancient relics and save Eldoria from the encroaching darkness."

Eldrin studied them for a moment, his eyes narrowing. "The relics, you say? And what makes you think you are worthy of such a quest?"

Kael stepped forward, his expression serious. "We have faced many challenges already, and we are prepared to face many more. We seek only to restore the magic and protect our land."

Lyra, ever the pragmatist, added, "And we could use all the help we can get."

Eldrin's gaze softened slightly, and he nodded. "Very well. Come, sit by the fire. There is much we must discuss."

They followed Eldrin to a small clearing where a fire crackled warmly. As they sat, Eldrin began to speak, his voice filled with the weight of centuries of knowledge.

"The prophecy of the Last Enchanter is ancient, passed down through generations. It speaks of five relics, each imbued with powerful magic. Together, they can restore the balance and drive back the darkness. But the path to finding them is fraught with danger."

Elara listened intently, her heart pounding with anticipation. "We have already learned of the Amulet of Light, hidden in the Lost City. What more can you tell us?"

Eldrin nodded. "The Amulet of Light is indeed the first relic. It is said to be guarded by powerful enchantments and creatures of the dark. But there are other relics—the Sword of Dawn, the Shield of Eternity, the Crown of Stars, and the Staff of Wisdom. Each one is hidden in a different part of Eldoria, protected by ancient magic."

Kael leaned forward, his eyes filled with determination. "We will find them. We have to."

Eldrin smiled, a glimmer of hope in his eyes. "I believe you will. And I will help you in any way I can. My knowledge of the ancient magic and the relics will be at your disposal."

Lyra, ever the practical one, asked, "And what about the dark mage? We've heard he seeks the relics as well."

Eldrin's expression grew serious. "The dark mage is a formidable foe. He seeks to control the relics and bend their power to his will. You must be vigilant and prepared for anything."

Elara nodded, her resolve hardening. "We will be. Thank you, Eldrin. Your wisdom is invaluable."

With Eldrin's guidance and knowledge, the trio felt a renewed sense of purpose. They had gained a powerful ally, and their quest to find the relics and save Eldoria was clearer than ever. As they prepared to leave the grove, Eldrin placed a hand on Elara's shoulder.

"Remember, the path ahead will be difficult, but you are not alone. Trust in each other, and you will succeed."

Elara smiled, her heart filled with gratitude. "Thank you, Eldrin. We won't let you down."

With their new ally by their side, Elara, Kael, and Lyra set off once more, their spirits high and their determination unwavering. The journey ahead would be long and perilous, but they were ready to face whatever challenges lay in their path. Together, they would gather the allies they needed and fight to save Eldoria from the encroaching darkness.

The Mountain Pass

The sun was just beginning to rise as Elara, Kael, Lyra, and Eldrin set off from the ancient grove. The air was crisp and cool, the forest alive with the sounds of morning. They moved with purpose, their steps quick and sure as they followed the path towards the mountains. The journey to the Lost City would take them through a treacherous mountain pass, a place known for its unpredictable weather and dangerous terrain.

As they approached the base of the mountains, the path grew steeper and more rugged. The trees thinned, giving way to rocky outcrops and narrow ledges. The air grew colder, and a biting wind whipped through the pass, carrying with it the scent of snow.

"We need to be careful," Kael said, his eyes scanning the path ahead. "This pass is known for sudden storms and rockslides."

Elara nodded, her grip tightening on her staff. "We'll need to stay close and watch each other's backs."

They began the ascent, their progress slow but steady. The path wound its way up the mountainside, the ground uneven and treacherous. Loose rocks shifted beneath their feet, and the wind howled around them, making it difficult to hear anything else.

As they climbed higher, dark clouds began to gather overhead, casting a shadow over the pass. The wind picked up, and the first flakes of snow began to fall, swirling around them in a blinding flurry.

"We need to find shelter," Eldrin shouted over the roar of the wind. "This storm is only going to get worse."

They pressed on, their eyes searching for any sign of a cave or overhang where they could take refuge. The snow fell thicker and faster, obscuring their vision and making the path even more treacherous.

Suddenly, a loud rumble echoed through the pass, and the ground beneath them began to shake. Rocks tumbled down the mountainside, crashing onto the path and sending up clouds of dust and debris.

"Rockslide!" Kael shouted, grabbing Elara's arm and pulling her to safety.

They scrambled to avoid the falling rocks, their hearts pounding with fear. Lyra darted ahead, her quick reflexes allowing her to dodge the debris with ease. Eldrin used his magic to create a protective barrier, shielding them from the worst of the rockslide.

When the dust finally settled, they found themselves on a narrow ledge, the path ahead blocked by a massive pile of rocks. The storm raged on, the wind howling and the snow falling in thick, blinding sheets.

"We can't stay here," Elara said, her voice trembling with cold. "We need to find another way."

Kael nodded, his eyes scanning the mountainside. "There," he said, pointing to a narrow path that wound its way up the side of the mountain. "It looks dangerous, but it's our only option."

They carefully made their way to the narrow path, their steps slow and cautious. The wind whipped around them, threatening to knock them off balance. The path was barely wide enough for one person, and the drop on either side was dizzying.

As they inched their way along the path, they heard a shout from above. Looking up, they saw a figure standing on a rocky outcrop, his cloak billowing in the wind. He was a tall, rugged man with a bow slung over his shoulder and a determined look in his eyes.

"Need some help?" he called out, his voice carrying over the wind.

Elara nodded, relief flooding through her. "Yes, please!"

The man made his way down to them with the ease of someone who knew the mountains well. He extended a hand to Elara, helping her over a particularly narrow section of the path.

"Name's Thorne," he said, his grip strong and steady. "I've been tracking the storm and saw you struggling. This pass can be deadly in weather like this."

"We're grateful for your help," Kael said, shaking Thorne's hand. "We're on a quest to find the ancient relics and save Eldoria from the encroaching darkness."

Thorne raised an eyebrow, his interest piqued. "Ancient relics, huh? Sounds like quite the adventure."

Elara nodded. "It is. And we could use someone with your skills. Will you join us?"

Thorne considered for a moment, his eyes scanning the group. "Alright," he said finally. "I'll help you navigate the pass. But once we're through, we'll see about this quest of yours."

With Thorne leading the way, they continued their ascent, the storm still raging around them. Thorne's knowledge of the mountains proved invaluable, guiding them safely through the treacherous terrain.

By the time they reached a sheltered overhang, the storm had begun to subside. They made camp, grateful for the respite from the wind and snow. As they sat around the fire, Thorne shared stories of his time in the mountains, his knowledge and experience adding a new layer of strength to their group.

Elara felt a renewed sense of hope. They had faced another challenge and emerged stronger for it. With Thorne by their side, they were one step closer to finding the relics and saving Eldoria. The journey ahead would be long and difficult, but together, they would face whatever challenges lay in their path.

The Enchanted Forest

The sun was high in the sky as Elara, Kael, Lyra, Eldrin, and Thorne made their way down the mountain pass. The storm had passed, leaving the air crisp and clear. They moved with renewed purpose, their steps quick and sure as they followed the path towards the Enchanted Forest.

The forest loomed ahead, its trees towering and ancient. The air was thick with magic, and the leaves shimmered with an ethereal glow. As they entered the forest, the sounds of the outside world faded away, replaced by the soft rustle of leaves and the distant calls of mystical creatures.

"This place is incredible," Lyra whispered, her eyes wide with wonder. "I've never seen anything like it."

Eldrin nodded, his expression serious. "The Enchanted Forest is a place of great power. But it is also a place of great danger. We must be cautious."

They moved deeper into the forest, the path winding through dense underbrush and towering trees. The air grew cooler, and a faint mist clung to the ground, giving the forest an otherworldly feel. As they walked, they began to notice strange things—trees that seemed to move, shadows that flickered at the edge of their vision, and whispers that seemed to come from nowhere.

"Stay close," Kael said, his hand resting on the hilt of his sword. "We don't know what we're dealing with here."

Suddenly, the path opened up into a large clearing. In the center stood a massive tree, its branches reaching towards the sky. The tree radiated a powerful, ancient magic, and Elara knew they had found the heart of the Enchanted Forest.

As they approached the tree, a figure stepped out from the shadows. She was tall and graceful, her hair flowing like liquid silver, her eyes glowing with an inner light. She wore a gown of leaves and flowers, and her presence seemed to make the very air shimmer.

"Welcome, travelers," she said, her voice like the rustle of leaves. "I am Aeliana, guardian of the Enchanted Forest. What brings you to my domain?"

Elara stepped forward, her head bowed in respect. "We seek the ancient relics to save Eldoria from the encroaching darkness. We have come to ask for your help."

Aeliana studied them for a moment, her eyes piercing and wise. "The relics are powerful, and the path to finding them is fraught with danger. But I sense that your intentions are pure. However, before I can offer my aid, you must prove your worthiness."

She raised her hand, and the ground beneath them began to tremble. The clearing transformed, and each member of the group found themselves facing a personal trial.

Elara stood in a darkened forest, the trees closing in around her. She could hear the whispers of the shadows, taunting her, trying to break her resolve. She took a deep breath, centering herself, and called upon her magic. A beam of light shot from her staff, dispelling the shadows and revealing a path forward.

Kael found himself on a battlefield, surrounded by ene-mies. His sword felt heavy in his hand, and doubt gnawed at his mind. But he remembered his training, his purpose, and fought with renewed strength. Each swing of his sword was precise and powerful, and he emerged victorious.

Lyra stood in a maze of mirrors, each reflection showing a different version of herself. She felt lost, unsure of who she truly was. But she remembered her skills, her quick wit, and used her daggers to shatter the mirrors, revealing the true path.

Eldrin faced a vision of his past, the mistakes he had made, the people he had lost. The weight of his years pressed down on him, but he remembered the wisdom he had gained, the knowledge he could share. He embraced his past, and the vision faded.

Thorne stood at the edge of a cliff, the wind howling around him. He felt the pull of the void, the temptation to give in to despair. But he remembered his duty, his strength, and took a step forward, finding solid ground beneath his feet.

When the trials were over, they found themselves back in the clearing, Aeliana standing before them. She smiled, her eyes filled with approval.

"You have proven your worthiness," she said. "I will join you on your quest. My knowledge of the forest and my magic will aid you in your journey."

Elara felt a surge of gratitude and hope. With Aeliana by their side, they were stronger than ever. The journey ahead would be long and difficult, but they were ready to face whatever challenges lay in their path. Together, they would gather the allies they needed and fight to save Eldoria from the encroaching darkness.

The Lost City

The sun was setting as Elara, Kael, Lyra, Eldrin, Thorne, and Aeliana approached the outskirts of the Lost City. The ancient ruins loomed ahead, their crumbling walls and towering spires casting long shadows in the fading light. The air was thick with the scent of moss and decay, and a sense of foreboding hung over the group.

"We should make camp here," Kael suggested, his eyes scanning the ruins for any signs of danger. "It's too risky to enter the city at night."

Elara nodded in agreement. "We'll need to be at our best to face whatever lies within. Let's rest and prepare for tomorrow."

They set up camp just outside the city, the flickering fire casting a warm glow on their faces. As they settled in for the night, the group gathered around the fire, their expressions a mix of determination and apprehension.

Eldrin produced a small, worn map from his satchel, spreading it out on the ground. "This map shows the layout of the Lost City," he explained. "The Amulet of Light is said to be hidden in the central temple, but the path to it is fraught with traps and guardians."

Lyra leaned in, her eyes scanning the map. "We'll need to be careful. The dark mage will likely have set his own traps to deter us."

Thorne nodded, his expression serious. "We'll need to move quickly and quietly. The element of surprise will be our greatest advantage."

Aeliana, her eyes glowing softly in the firelight, added, "The magic of the forest will aid us. I can sense the presence of the guardians, and I will guide us through the traps."

Elara felt a surge of gratitude for her companions. Each of them brought unique skills and knowledge to the group, and together, they were stronger than ever. "We'll face whatever challenges lie ahead," she said, her voice filled with determination. "Together, we will find the Amulet of Light and save Eldoria."

As the night wore on, they shared stories and strengthened their bonds. Kael spoke of his time as a warrior, fighting to protect his homeland. Lyra recounted tales of her adventures as a rogue thief, her quick wit and sharp reflexes saving her from countless dangers. Eldrin shared his wisdom and knowledge of ancient magic, while Thorne spoke of his time in the mountains, his skills as a ranger honed by years of survival.

Aeliana, her voice like the rustle of leaves, told stories of the Enchanted Forest and the creatures that dwelled within. Her presence brought a sense of calm and serenity to the group, and Elara felt a deep connection to the guardian of the forest.

As the fire burned low, Elara looked around at her companions, her heart filled with hope. They had come a long way since leaving Eldenwood, and the journey ahead would be even more challenging. But with their combined strength and determination, she knew they could succeed.

"We should rest," Kael said, his voice gentle but firm. "We'll need all our strength for tomorrow."

They settled down for the night, each taking turns to keep watch. Elara lay beneath the stars, her mind racing with thoughts of the prophecy and the journey ahead. She knew the path would be fraught with danger, but she was ready to face it.

In the quiet of the night, Elara felt a sense of peace. The prophecy had brought them together, and together, they would fight to save Eldoria. She closed her eyes, letting the sounds of the forest lull her to sleep, her heart filled with hope and determination.

The dawn broke with a soft, golden light, casting a warm glow over the ruins of the Lost City. Elara and her companions packed up their camp and prepared to enter the city, their spirits high and their resolve unwavering.

As they approached the entrance to the central temple, Elara felt a surge of excitement and anticipation. The journey ahead would be long and difficult, but they were ready to face whatever challenges lay in their path. Together, they would find the Amulet of Light and save Eldoria from the encroaching darkness.

Chapter 4: The Hidden Library

Discovery of the Library

The sun was just beginning to rise as Elara, Kael, Lyra, Eldrin, Thorne, and Aeliana approached the outskirts of the ancient, overgrown city. The ruins loomed ahead, their crumbling walls and towering spires shrouded in a thick blanket of ivy and moss. The air was heavy with the scent of damp earth and decaying leaves, and a sense of anticipation hung over the group.

"This is it," Eldrin said, his voice filled with awe. "The hidden library is somewhere within these ruins."

Elara nodded, her eyes scanning the overgrown city. "We need to be careful. The library is likely protected by traps and magical wards."

They split up to search the ruins, each member of the group taking a different section. Elara moved cautiously through the crumbling streets, her staff glowing softly to light her way. The buildings were in various states of decay, their walls covered in thick vines and their windows shattered.

As she rounded a corner, she spotted a wall of enchanted vines, their leaves shimmering with a faint, magical glow. Elara approached cautiously, her heart pounding with excitement. She reached out to touch the vines, feeling the magic thrumming beneath her fingertips.

"Over here!" she called out, her voice echoing through the ruins.

The rest of the group quickly joined her, their eyes widening as they took in the sight of the enchanted vines. "This must be the entrance," Kael said, his hand resting on the hilt of his sword.

Elara nodded. "We need to dispel the enchantments to gain entry."

Aeliana stepped forward, her eyes glowing with a soft, inner light. "I can help with that."

Together, Elara and Aeliana began to chant a series of incantations, their voices blending harmoniously. The vines shivered and began to unravel, revealing a hidden doorway behind them. The air was thick with magic, and Elara could feel the power of the library just beyond the door.

With a final, powerful incantation, the last of the vines fell away, and the doorway stood open before them. Elara took a deep breath, her heart pounding with anticipation. "Let's go."

They stepped through the doorway and into the hidden library. The air inside was cool and dry, filled with the scent of old parchment and dust. The library was vast, its shelves stretching up to the high, vaulted ceiling. Ancient tomes and artifacts filled the shelves, their covers worn and faded with age.

"This place is incredible," Lyra whispered, her eyes wide with wonder. "I've never seen so many books in one place."

Eldrin nodded, his expression serious. "We need to find information on the relics. Spread out and search the shelves. Be careful—there may be traps."

They moved through the library, each member of the group focusing on a different section. Elara ran her fingers along the spines of the books, her eyes scanning the titles for anything that might be useful. The library was a treasure trove of knowledge, and she knew they were on the brink of a major discovery.

As she reached the end of a row of shelves, Elara spotted a small, ornate box tucked away in a corner. She carefully lifted the lid, revealing a series of scrolls inside. Her heart raced as she unrolled one of the scrolls, her eyes widening as she read the ancient script.

"Eldrin, come look at this," she called out, her voice trembling with excitement.

Eldrin hurried over, his eyes scanning the scroll. "These are records of the relics," he said, his voice filled with awe. "This could be exactly what we need."

As they continued to search the library, Lyra suddenly cried out in alarm. "Watch out!"

Elara turned just in time to see a magical trap spring to life, a series of glowing runes lighting up on the floor. She raised her staff, chanting a quick incantation to dispel the trap. The runes flickered and died, and the danger passed.

"Be careful," Kael warned, his eyes scanning the floor for any more traps. "We can't afford any mistakes."

With renewed caution, they continued their search, determined to uncover the secrets of the hidden library. The journey ahead would be long and difficult, but they were ready to face whatever challenges lay in their path. Together, they would find the relics and save Eldoria from the encroaching darkness.

Exploring the Library

The hidden library was a marvel of ancient architecture, its vast halls filled with rows upon rows of towering bookshelves. The air was thick with the scent of old parchment and dust, and the faint glow of magical orbs provided a soft, ambient light. Elara, Kael, Lyra, Eldrin, Thorne, and Aeliana stood in awe, taking in the sheer magnitude of the knowledge contained within these walls.

"This place is incredible," Lyra whispered, her voice echoing softly in the cavernous space. "I've never seen so many books in one place."

Eldrin nodded, his eyes scanning the shelves. "We need to find information on the relics. Spread out and search the shelves. Be careful—there may be traps."

The group dispersed, each member heading to a different section of the library. Elara moved cautiously through the aisles, her fingers trailing along the spines of the books. She could feel the magic thrumming in the air, a testament to the power and knowledge contained within these ancient tomes.

As she reached the end of a row of shelves, Elara spotted a small, ornate box tucked away in a corner. She carefully lifted the lid, revealing a series of scrolls inside. Her heart raced as she unrolled one of the scrolls, her eyes widening as she read the ancient script.

"Eldrin, come look at this," she called out, her voice trembling with excitement.

Eldrin hurried over, his eyes scanning the scroll. "These are records of the relics," he said, his voice filled with awe. "This could be exactly what we need."

Meanwhile, Kael was searching through a section filled with ancient artifacts. He carefully examined each item, looking for anything that might provide a clue to the locations of the relics. His eyes fell on a dusty old book, its cover adorned with intricate runes. He opened it, revealing pages filled with detailed illustrations and descriptions of the relics.

"Elara, I think I've found something," Kael called out, holding up the book.

Elara and Eldrin joined him, their eyes scanning the pages. "This is incredible," Elara said, her voice filled with wonder. "These illustrations match the descriptions in the scrolls. We're on the right track."

As they continued to search, Lyra moved through the aisles with her usual grace and agility. She was drawn to a section filled with ancient maps and charts. Her eyes lit up as she found a map that seemed to detail the locations of the relics.

"Hey, over here!" Lyra called out, holding up the map. "I think I've found something important."

The group gathered around, their eyes scanning the map. "This shows the locations of the relics," Eldrin said, his voice filled with excitement. "We need to study this carefully."

As they pored over the map, Lyra suddenly felt a chill run down her spine. She turned just in time to see a series of glowing runes light up on the floor beneath her feet. "Watch out!" she cried, leaping back as a magical trap sprang to life.

Elara raised her staff, chanting a quick incantation to dispel the trap. The runes flickered and died, and the danger passed. "Be careful," Kael warned, his eyes scanning the floor for any more traps. "We can't afford any mistakes."

With renewed caution, they continued their search, determined to uncover the secrets of the hidden library. The journey ahead would be long and difficult, but they were ready to face whatever challenges lay in their path. Together, they would find the relics and save Eldoria from the encroaching darkness.

As they delved deeper into the library, they uncovered more clues and pieces of the puzzle. Eldrin found a series of scrolls that detailed the history of the relics and their locations. Kael discovered an ancient artifact that seemed to resonate with the magic of the library. Lyra found more maps and charts, each one providing valuable information about their quest.

The group worked tirelessly, their determination unwavering. They knew that the knowledge contained within the hidden library was the key to their success. With each new discovery, their resolve grew stronger, and their bond as a team deepened.

As the hours passed, they finally gathered all the information they needed. Eldrin carefully rolled up the scrolls and placed them in his satchel. Kael secured the ancient artifact, and Lyra folded the maps and charts.

"We've found everything we need," Elara said, her voice filled with determination. "Now, we must prepare for the next stage of our journey."

With their newfound knowledge and a renewed sense of purpose, the group prepared to leave the hidden library. The journey ahead would be long and difficult, but they were ready to face whatever challenges lay in their path. Together, they would find the relics and save Eldoria from the encroaching darkness.

The Dark Mage's Presence

The hidden library was a labyrinth of knowledge, its vast halls filled with ancient tomes and artifacts. As Elara, Kael, Lyra, Eldrin, Thorne, and Aeliana continued their search, a sense of unease began to settle over them. The air grew colder, and the shadows seemed to lengthen, as if the very walls were watching them.

Elara paused, her eyes scanning the shelves. "Do you feel that?" she asked, her voice barely above a whisper. "It's as if someone—or something—is here with us."

Kael nodded, his hand resting on the hilt of his sword. "I feel it too. We need to be on our guard."

As they moved deeper into the library, they began to notice signs that someone else had been there recently. Books were out of place, scrolls were unrolled, and a faint, acrid smell lingered in the air.

"This isn't right," Lyra muttered, her eyes darting around the room. "Someone's been here, and it wasn't us."

Eldrin's expression grew serious. "The dark mage. He must have sent his minions to guard the library and prevent us from finding the relics."

Aeliana's eyes glowed with a soft, inner light. "We must be cautious. The dark mage's presence is strong here."

Suddenly, a low growl echoed through the library, and the group spun around to see a pack of dark creatures emerging from the shadows. Their eyes glowed with a malevolent light, and their claws scraped against the stone floor.

"Get ready," Kael said, drawing his sword. "Here they come."

The creatures lunged at them, their movements swift and deadly. Kael met them head-on, his sword flashing in the dim light as he cut down the first wave of attackers. Elara raised her staff, chanting a spell that sent a wave of light through the room, driving back the creatures.

Lyra moved with her usual grace and agility, her daggers flashing as she took down one creature after another. Thorne's arrows flew true, each one finding its mark with deadly precision. Eldrin used his magic to create protective barriers, shielding the group from the worst of the attacks.

Aeliana's presence was a calming force, her magic weaving through the air like a gentle breeze. She summoned vines from the ground, entangling the creatures and holding them in place. Her eyes glowed with determination as she fought alongside her companions.

The battle was fierce, the air filled with the sounds of clashing metal and snarling creatures. The group fought with everything they had, their skills and teamwork tested to the limit. But they were determined to succeed, to protect the knowledge contained within the library and continue their quest.

As the last of the creatures fell, the library fell silent once more. The group stood panting, their weapons at the ready, their eyes scanning the room for any remaining threats.

"We did it," Elara said, her voice filled with relief. "But we need to be careful. The dark mage knows we're here, and he'll stop at nothing to prevent us from finding the relics."

Kael nodded, his expression serious. "We need to move quickly. Let's gather what we need and get out of here."

They continued their search, their movements quick and efficient. Eldrin found a series of scrolls that detailed the history of the relics and their locations. Kael discovered an ancient artifact that seemed to resonate with the magic of the library. Lyra found more maps and charts, each one providing valuable information about their quest.

As they gathered their findings, Elara couldn't shake the feeling of unease that lingered in the air. The dark mage's presence was strong, and she knew they would face even greater challenges in the days to come.

"We have what we need," Eldrin said, his voice filled with determination. "Let's get out of here."

With their newfound knowledge and a renewed sense of purpose, the group prepared to leave the hidden library.

The journey ahead would be long and difficult, but they were ready to face whatever challenges lay in their path. Together, they would find the relics and save Eldoria from the encroaching darkness.

The Hidden Chamber

The hidden library was a maze of knowledge, its vast halls filled with ancient tomes and artifacts. As Elara, Kael, Lyra, Eldrin, Thorne, and Aeliana continued their search, they felt the weight of the dark mage's presence lingering in the air. Despite their recent victory over the dark creatures, they knew their quest was far from over.

Elara moved cautiously through the aisles, her eyes scanning the shelves for any sign of further danger. As she reached the end of a row, she noticed a faint glow emanating from behind a large bookshelf. Her curiosity piqued, she approached the source of the light.

"Over here," she called softly to her companions. "I think I've found something."

The group gathered around, their eyes widening as they saw the glow. Eldrin stepped forward, his expression serious. "This could be a hidden chamber. The library is known for its secrets."

Aeliana nodded, her eyes glowing with a soft, inner light. "I can sense powerful enchantments protecting this area. We must be careful."

Together, they began to examine the bookshelf, searching for any clues that might reveal the entrance to the hidden chamber. Lyra's keen eyes spotted a series of runes etched into the wood, their lines faint but unmistakable.

"These runes are a key," she said, tracing her fingers over the symbols. "We need to activate them in the correct sequence to open the door."

Eldrin studied the runes, his brow furrowed in concentration. "These are ancient symbols, used by the Enchanters to protect their most valuable secrets. Let me see if I can decipher them."

As Eldrin worked to decode the runes, Elara and Aeliana prepared to dispel the enchantments. The air around them crackled with magic, the power of the library resonating with their own.

"Ready?" Elara asked, her voice steady.

Aeliana nodded. "Let's do this."

With a series of precise movements, Eldrin activated the runes, each symbol lighting up with a soft glow. Elara and Aeliana chanted a series of incantations, their voices blending harmoniously as they worked to dispel the enchantments.

The bookshelf shuddered and began to move, revealing a hidden doorway behind it. The air was thick with magic, and Elara could feel the power of the hidden chamber just beyond the door.

"Let's go," Kael said, his hand resting on the hilt of his sword.

They stepped through the doorway and into the hidden chamber. The room was filled with a soft, golden light, its walls lined with shelves of ancient texts and artifacts. In the center of the room stood a large, ornate table, covered in scrolls and maps.

"This is incredible," Lyra whispered, her eyes wide with wonder. "I've never seen anything like it."

Eldrin approached the table, his eyes scanning the scrolls. "These are records of the relics," he said, his voice filled with awe. "This could be exactly what we need."

As they examined the contents of the chamber, Elara's eyes fell on a detailed map of Eldoria, marked with symbols and runes. Her heart raced as she realized what it was.

"This map shows the locations of the relics," she said, her voice trembling with excitement. "We have everything we need to continue our quest."

Eldrin carefully unrolled a scroll, his eyes scanning the ancient script. "This scroll contains a crucial piece of the prophecy," he said, his voice filled with determination. "It reveals the next steps in our journey."

As they gathered the most important texts and artifacts, Elara felt a renewed sense of purpose. They had uncovered valuable information that would guide them on their quest to find the relics and save Eldoria.

"We've found everything we need," Kael said, his voice filled with determination. "Let's get out of here."

With their newfound knowledge and a renewed sense of purpose, the group prepared to leave the hidden library. The journey ahead would be long and difficult, but they were ready to face whatever challenges lay in their path. Together, they would find the relics and save Eldoria from the encroaching darkness.

Departure and Reflection

The hidden chamber was a treasure trove of ancient knowledge, its shelves filled with scrolls and artifacts that held the secrets of Eldoria's past. Elara, Kael, Lyra, Eldrin, Thorne, and Aeliana worked quickly, gathering the most important texts and maps. The air was thick with the scent of old parchment and the faint hum of residual magic.

"We've found everything we need," Eldrin said, carefully rolling up a scroll and placing it in his satchel. "This information will be invaluable in our quest."

Kael nodded, his expression serious. "We should leave before the dark mage sends more of his minions. We can't afford to be caught off guard."

Elara agreed, her heart pounding with a mix of excitement and apprehension. They had uncovered crucial information about the relics and the prophecy, but the journey ahead would be fraught with danger. "Let's get out of here," she said, her voice steady.

They made their way back through the library, their movements quick and efficient. The shadows seemed to watch them as they passed, a reminder of the dark mage's presence. But Elara felt a renewed sense of purpose, bolstered by the knowledge they had gained.

As they stepped out into the cool night air, the ruins of the ancient city loomed around them, bathed in the soft glow of the moon. They set up camp just outside the library, the flickering fire casting a warm light on their faces.

"We've come a long way," Lyra said, her voice thoughtful as she stared into the flames. "But the hardest part is still ahead of us."

Thorne nodded, his eyes reflecting the firelight. "The dark mage won't stop until he has the relics. We need to be ready for anything."

Aeliana's presence was a calming force, her eyes glowing softly in the darkness. "We have each other," she said, her voice like the rustle of leaves. "Together, we are strong."

Elara felt a surge of gratitude for her companions. Each of them brought unique skills and knowledge to the group, and together, they were a formidable team. "We've faced many challenges already," she said, her voice filled with determination. "And we'll face many more. But I believe in us. We can do this."

Eldrin smiled, his eyes filled with wisdom. "The prophecy speaks of the Last Enchanter and the allies who will stand by their side. We are those allies. And we will succeed."

As they sat around the fire, they shared stories and strengthened their bonds. Kael spoke of his time as a warrior, fighting to protect his homeland. Lyra recounted tales of her adventures as a rogue thief, her quick wit and sharp reflexes saving her from countless dangers. Eldrin shared his wisdom and knowledge of ancient magic, while Thorne spoke of his time in the mountains, his skills as a ranger honed by years of survival.

Aeliana, her voice like a gentle breeze, told stories of the Enchanted Forest and the creatures that dwelled within. Her presence brought a sense of calm and serenity to the group, and Elara felt a deep connection to the guardian of the forest.

As the fire burned low, Elara looked around at her companions, her heart filled with hope. They had come a long way since leaving Eldenwood, and the journey ahead would be even more challenging. But with their combined strength and determination, she knew they could succeed.

"We should rest," Kael said, his voice gentle but firm. "We'll need all our strength for the journey ahead."

They settled down for the night, each taking turns to keep watch. Elara lay beneath the stars, her mind racing with thoughts of the prophecy and the challenges that awaited them. She knew the path would be fraught with danger, but she was ready to face it.

In the quiet of the night, Elara felt a sense of peace. The prophecy had brought them together, and together, they would fight to save Eldoria. She closed her eyes, letting the sounds of the forest lull her to sleep, her heart filled with hope and determination.

The dawn broke with a soft, golden light, casting a warm glow over the ruins of the ancient city. Elara and her companions packed up their camp and prepared to continue their journey, their spirits high and their resolve unwavering.

As they set off towards their next destination, Elara felt a surge of excitement and anticipation. The journey ahead would be long and difficult, but they were ready to face whatever challenges lay in their path. Together, they would find the relics and save Eldoria from the encroaching darkness.

Chapter 5: Trials and Tribulations

The First Trial

The sun was just beginning to rise as Elara, Kael, Lyra, Eldrin, Thorne, and Aeliana approached the entrance to a mystical cave. The air was crisp and cool, the forest around them alive with the sounds of morning. The cave loomed ahead, its entrance shrouded in shadows and covered in ancient runes that glowed faintly in the dim light.

"This is it," Eldrin said, his voice filled with awe. "The first trial site. The Amulet of Light is said to be hidden within."

Elara nodded, her heart pounding with anticipation. "We need to be careful. The cave is likely filled with traps and puzzles designed to test us."

Kael drew his sword, his eyes scanning the entrance. "Let's stick together and watch each other's backs."

They stepped into the cave, the air growing cooler and the light dimmer as they moved deeper inside. The walls were covered in intricate carvings, depicting scenes of ancient battles and powerful magic. The runes glowed brighter as they passed, casting an eerie light on their path.

As they ventured further, they came upon the first of many challenges—a series of magical traps and puzzles. The floor was covered in tiles, each one inscribed with a different symbol. Eldrin knelt down, studying the symbols carefully.

"These symbols represent different elements," he said, his voice thoughtful. "We need to step on the tiles in the correct order to deactivate the trap."

Lyra raised an eyebrow. "And how do we know the correct order?"

Eldrin smiled, his eyes twinkling with excitement. "We use our knowledge and intuition. The elements must be balanced—fire, water, earth, and air."

They worked together, carefully stepping on the tiles in the correct order. The trap deactivated with a soft click, and they moved forward, their confidence growing with each success. But the challenges grew more difficult as they progressed, testing their intelligence and teamwork.

At one point, they encountered a puzzle that required them to manipulate a series of levers and gears to open a door. Tensions rose as they struggled to solve the puzzle, revealing underlying fears and doubts.

"This isn't working," Kael said, his frustration evident. "We're missing something."

Elara took a deep breath, trying to calm her racing thoughts. "We need to think logically. Each lever controls a different gear. We need to find the right combination."

Lyra's eyes narrowed as she studied the puzzle. "What if we try this?" she suggested, moving one of the levers to a different position.

The gears clicked into place, and the door creaked open. The group let out a collective sigh of relief, their spirits lifting as they moved forward.

As they navigated the cave, they encountered more traps and puzzles, each one more challenging than the last. But through their combined efforts and mutual support, they overcame each obstacle, their bond growing stronger with each success.

Finally, they reached the heart of the cave, where the Amulet of Light was said to be hidden. The chamber was bathed in a soft, golden light, and in the center stood a pedestal, upon which rested the amulet. Its surface shimmered with a radiant glow, casting a warm light on their faces.

"We did it," Elara said, her voice filled with awe. "We found the first relic."

Kael stepped forward, his hand reaching out to take the amulet. "This is just the beginning. We have many more trials ahead of us."

As Kael lifted the amulet from the pedestal, the chamber filled with a blinding light. The runes on the walls glowed brightly, and the air hummed with magic. Elara felt a surge of energy, her heart swelling with hope and determination.

"We're one step closer to saving Eldoria," she said, her voice filled with resolve. "Let's keep moving."

With the Amulet of Light in their possession, the group made their way back through the cave, their spirits high and their resolve unwavering. They had faced their first trial and emerged victorious, their bond stronger than ever.

The journey ahead would be long and difficult, but they were ready to face whatever challenges lay in their path. Together, they would find the relics and save Eldoria from the encroaching darkness.

The Guardian's Challenge

The group emerged from the mystical cave, the Amulet of Light safely in their possession. The sun was high in the sky, casting a warm glow over the forest. They moved with renewed purpose, their steps quick and sure as they followed the path towards the sacred grove, the site of their next trial.

The grove was a place of ancient magic, its trees towering and ancient. The air was thick with the scent of pine and earth, and a faint mist clung to the ground, giving the forest an otherworldly feel. As they approached the grove, they could feel the power of the place, a palpable energy that thrummed in the air.

"This is it," Eldrin said, his voice filled with awe. "The second trial awaits us here."

Elara nodded, her heart pounding with anticipation. "We need to be prepared. The guardian of this grove is said to be a powerful elemental spirit."

They stepped into the grove, the air growing cooler and the light dimmer as they moved deeper inside. The trees seemed to close in around them, their branches intertwining to form a canopy that blocked out the sun. The ground was covered in a thick carpet of moss, and the air was filled with the sound of rustling leaves.

As they ventured further, they came upon a clearing. In the center stood a massive tree, its branches reaching towards the sky. The tree radiated a powerful, ancient magic, and Elara knew they had found the heart of the grove.

Suddenly, the air around them shimmered, and a figure appeared before them. The guardian of the grove was a tall, graceful being, her hair flowing like liquid silver, her eyes glowing with an inner light. She wore a gown of leaves and flowers, and her presence seemed to make the very air shimmer.

"Welcome, travelers," she said, her voice like the rustle of leaves. "I am Sylphara, guardian of this grove. You seek the second relic, but first, you must prove your worthiness."

Elara stepped forward, her head bowed in respect. "We are ready to face the trial."

Sylphara nodded, her eyes scanning the group. "Each of you must face a personal trial, confronting your deepest fears and insecurities. Only then will you be deemed worthy of the relic."

With a wave of her hand, the clearing transformed, and each member of the group found themselves facing a personal trial.

Elara stood in a darkened forest, the trees closing in around her. She could hear the whispers of the shadows, taunting her, trying to break her resolve. She took a deep breath, centering herself, and called upon her magic. A beam of light shot from her staff, dispelling the shadows and revealing a path forward.

Kael found himself on a battlefield, surrounded by enemies. His sword felt heavy in his hand, and doubt gnawed at his mind. But he remembered his training, his purpose, and fought with renewed strength. Each swing of his sword was precise and powerful, and he emerged victorious.

Lyra stood in a maze of mirrors, each reflection showing a different version of herself. She felt lost, unsure of who she truly was. But she remembered her skills, her quick wit, and used her daggers to shatter the mirrors, revealing the true path.

Eldrin faced a vision of his past, the mistakes he had made, the people he had lost. The weight of his years pressed down on him, but he remembered the wisdom he had gained, the knowledge he could share. He embraced his past, and the vision faded.

Thorne stood at the edge of a cliff, the wind howling around him. He felt the pull of the void, the temptation to give in to despair. But he remembered his duty, his strength, and took a step forward, finding solid ground beneath his feet.

When the trials were over, they found themselves back in the clearing, Sylphara standing before them. She smiled, her eyes filled with approval.

"You have proven your worthiness," she said. "The second relic is yours."

She raised her hand, and a small, ornate box appeared before them. Inside was a beautiful, glowing crystal, its surface shimmering with a radiant light.

"This is the Crystal of Clarity," Sylphara said. "It will guide you on your journey and help you see through the darkness."

Elara took the crystal, her heart swelling with gratitude. "Thank you, Sylphara. We will use it wisely."

With the second relic in their possession, the group felt a renewed sense of purpose. They had faced their deepest fears and emerged stronger for it. The journey ahead would be long and difficult, but they were ready to face whatever challenges lay in their path. Together, they would find the relics and save Eldoria from the encroaching darkness.

The Betrayal

The group continued their journey with the Crystal of Clarity safely in their possession. The path led them to an ancient fortress, its towering walls and crumbling battlements a testament to the battles fought there long ago. The air was thick with the scent of moss and decay, and a sense of foreboding hung over the group.

"This is the site of the third trial," Eldrin said, his voice echoing softly in the stillness. "The third relic is hidden within the heart of this fortress."

Elara nodded, her heart pounding with anticipation. "We need to be careful. The dark mage's influence is strong here."

They approached the entrance to the fortress, the massive wooden doors creaking open with a groan. The interior was dark and foreboding, the walls lined with ancient tapestries and the floor covered in a thick layer of dust. The air was cool and damp, and the only sound was the soft echo of their footsteps.

As they ventured deeper into the fortress, they encountered a series of traps and obstacles, each one more challenging than the last. The dark mage's presence was palpable, his magic woven into the very fabric of the fortress.

"We need to stay focused," Kael said, his hand resting on the hilt of his sword. "The dark mage will do everything he can to stop us."

They moved cautiously through the fortress, their eyes scanning the shadows for any sign of danger. As they reached the central chamber, they found the third relic—a beautifully crafted shield, its surface adorned with intricate runes and symbols.

"This is the Shield of Eternity," Eldrin said, his voice filled with awe. "It is said to protect its bearer from any harm."

Elara stepped forward, her hand reaching out to take the shield. But as she did, a dark figure emerged from the shadows, his eyes glowing with a malevolent light.

"Stop right there," the figure said, his voice cold and menacing. "The shield belongs to me."

The group turned to face the intruder, their weapons at the ready. "Who are you?" Kael demanded, his sword drawn.

The figure stepped into the light, revealing himself to be one of their own—Thorne. His eyes were filled with a dark, twisted hunger, and his expression was one of triumph.

"Thorne, what are you doing?" Elara asked, her voice trembling with shock.

Thorne sneered, his hand resting on the hilt of his sword. "The dark mage has promised me power beyond my wildest dreams. All I have to do is deliver the relics to him."

Kael's eyes narrowed, his grip tightening on his sword. "You've betrayed us."

Thorne laughed, a cold, hollow sound. "You were fools to trust me. The dark mage's power is unmatched. With his help, I will become unstoppable."

Elara's heart ached with betrayal, but she knew they couldn't afford to let Thorne succeed. "We won't let you take the shield," she said, her voice filled with determination.

A fierce battle ensued, the air filled with the clash of metal and the crackle of magic. Thorne fought with a ferocity born of desperation, his attacks swift and deadly. But the group fought back with equal determination, their bond stronger than ever.

Kael's sword flashed in the dim light, each strike precise and powerful. Lyra moved with her usual grace and agility, her daggers finding their mark with deadly accuracy. Eldrin used his magic to create protective barriers, shielding the group from Thorne's attacks. Aeliana summoned vines from the ground, entangling Thorne and holding him in place.

Elara raised her staff, chanting a powerful incantation. A beam of light shot from her staff, striking Thorne and enveloping him in a shimmering aura. Thorne cried out in pain, his body writhing as the light purified the darkness within him.

With a final, agonized scream, Thorne collapsed to the ground, his eyes returning to their natural color. He lay there, breathing heavily, his expression one of defeat.

"I'm sorry," Thorne whispered, his voice filled with regret. "I was blinded by the dark mage's promises."

Elara knelt beside him, her hand resting on his shoulder. "It's not too late to make things right. Help us defeat the dark mage and save Eldoria."

Thorne nodded, his eyes filled with determination. "I will. I won't let the dark mage win."

With Thorne's betrayal behind them, the group reclaimed the Shield of Eternity and reaffirmed their commitment to their quest. The journey ahead would be long and difficult, but they were ready to face whatever challenges lay in their path. Together, they would find the relics and save Eldoria from the encroaching darkness.

The Trial of Strength

The group left the ancient fortress behind, the Shield of Eternity safely in their possession. Their journey led them to the base of a towering mountain, its peak shrouded in clouds. The air was thin and cold, and the path ahead was steep and treacherous. This was the site of their fourth trial, a test of their physical strength and endurance.

"We need to be prepared," Kael said, his eyes scanning the rocky terrain. "This trial will push us to our limits."

Elara nodded, her heart pounding with anticipation. "We need to stay together and support each other. The mountain will test our strength, but our unity will see us through."

They began their ascent, the path winding its way up the mountainside. The ground was uneven and covered in loose rocks, making each step a challenge. The wind howled around them, carrying with it the scent of snow and ice.

As they climbed higher, the air grew colder and the path more difficult. The group moved slowly, their muscles straining with the effort. The harsh conditions took a toll on them, causing tempers to flare and morale to waver.

"This is impossible," Lyra muttered, her breath coming in short gasps. "We'll never make it to the top."

Kael placed a reassuring hand on her shoulder. "We can do this. We just need to keep moving and support each other."

Eldrin, his face lined with determination, used his magic to create a protective barrier against the biting wind. "We must push through. The relic is within our reach."

Thorne, his betrayal still fresh in their minds, worked tirelessly to prove his loyalty. He led the way, his knowledge of the mountains guiding them through the most treacherous sections of the path.

Aeliana's presence was a calming force, her magic weaving through the air like a gentle breeze. She summoned vines to create handholds and footholds, making the climb a little easier for the group.

As they neared the peak, the path grew even more challenging. They encountered a series of physical obstacles—rock walls to climb, narrow ledges to traverse, and deep chasms to cross. Each challenge tested their strength, endurance, and resilience.

At one point, they came upon a sheer rock face, its surface slick with ice. Kael took the lead, his strong arms pulling him up the wall with practiced ease. Elara followed, her fingers numb with cold as she gripped the icy rock.

Lyra, her quick reflexes serving her well, moved with agility and grace. Eldrin used his magic to create footholds in the ice, while Thorne and Aeliana provided support from below.

As they reached the top of the rock face, they found themselves on a narrow ledge, the wind howling around them. The peak of the mountain was just ahead, but the final stretch was the most difficult.

"We're almost there," Elara said, her voice filled with determination. "We can do this."

With renewed resolve, they pushed forward, their bodies aching with the effort. The wind whipped around them, threatening to knock them off balance, but they held on, their eyes fixed on the peak.

Finally, they reached the summit, their breaths coming in ragged gasps. The view from the top was breathtaking, the landscape stretching out before them in a patchwork of snow and rock.

In the center of the peak stood a pedestal, upon which rested the fourth relic—a beautifully crafted sword, its blade shimmering with a radiant light.

"This is the Sword of Dawn," Eldrin said, his voice filled with awe. "It is said to grant its bearer unparalleled strength and courage."

Kael stepped forward, his hand reaching out to take the sword. As he lifted it from the pedestal, the air around them shimmered with magic, and the runes on the blade glowed brightly.

"We did it," Elara said, her voice filled with pride. "We faced the trial of strength and emerged victorious."

With the Sword of Dawn in their possession, the group felt a renewed sense of purpose. They had faced their physical limits and overcome them, their bond stronger than ever.

The journey ahead would be long and difficult, but they were ready to face whatever challenges lay in their path. Together, they would find the relics and save Eldoria from the encroaching darkness.

The Final Trial

The group descended from the mountain peak, the Sword of Dawn safely in their possession. Their journey led them to a hidden valley, a place shrouded in mystery and magic. The air was thick with anticipation, and the shadows seemed to whisper of the challenges that lay ahead. This was the site of their final trial, the last step in their quest to gather the relics.

As they approached the entrance to the valley, they could feel the dark mage's presence growing stronger. The ground was covered in a thick layer of mist, and the trees loomed overhead, their branches twisted and gnarled. The air was cold and still, and a sense of foreboding hung over the group.

"This is it," Eldrin said, his voice filled with determination. "The final trial awaits us here."

Elara nodded, her heart pounding with anticipation. "We need to be prepared. The dark mage's minions will be waiting for us."

Kael drew his sword, his eyes scanning the shadows. "Let's stick together and watch each other's backs."

They stepped into the valley, the air growing colder and the light dimmer as they moved deeper inside. The ground was uneven and covered in roots and rocks, making each step a challenge. The mist swirled around them, obscuring their vision and making it difficult to see what lay ahead.

As they ventured further, they came upon a clearing. In the center stood a massive stone altar, its surface covered in ancient runes and symbols. The final relic, a beautifully crafted staff, rested on the altar, its surface shimmering with a radiant light.

"This is the Staff of Wisdom," Eldrin said, his voice filled with awe. "It is said to grant its bearer unparalleled knowledge and insight."

Elara stepped forward, her hand reaching out to take the staff. But as she did, a dark figure emerged from the shadows, his eyes glowing with a malevolent light.

"Stop right there," the figure said, his voice cold and menacing. "The staff belongs to me."

The group turned to face the intruder, their weapons at the ready. The dark mage's minions emerged from the shadows, their eyes glowing with a sinister light. The air was filled with the sound of snarling and growling, and the ground trembled beneath their feet.

"Get ready," Kael said, his voice steady. "Here they come."

A fierce battle ensued, the air filled with the clash of metal and the crackle of magic. The dark mage's minions were swift and deadly, their attacks relentless. But the group fought back with equal determination, their bond stronger than ever.

Kael's sword flashed in the dim light, each strike precise and powerful. Lyra moved with her usual grace and agility, her daggers finding their mark with deadly accuracy. Eldrin used his magic to create protective barriers, shielding the group from the worst of the attacks. Thorne's arrows flew true, each one finding its mark with deadly precision. Aeliana summoned vines from the ground, entangling the minions and holding them in place.

Elara raised her staff, chanting a powerful incantation. A beam of light shot from her staff, striking the dark mage's minions and enveloping them in a shimmering aura. The minions cried out in pain, their bodies writhing as the light purified the darkness within them.

The battle was fierce and chaotic, each member of the group facing their own personal struggles. Kael fought with a ferocity born of desperation, his attacks swift and deadly. Lyra moved with agility and grace, her quick reflexes saving her from countless dangers. Eldrin used his magic to create protective barriers, shielding the group from the worst of the attacks. Thorne's arrows flew true, each one finding its mark with deadly precision. Aeliana's presence was a calming force, her magic weaving through the air like a gentle breeze.

As the last of the dark mage's minions fell, the valley fell silent once more. The group stood panting, their weapons at the ready, their eyes scanning the clearing for any remaining threats.

"We did it," Elara said, her voice filled with relief. "But we need to be careful. The dark mage knows we're here, and he'll stop at nothing to prevent us from finding the relics."

Kael nodded, his expression serious. "We need to move quickly. Let's gather the staff and get out of here."

Elara stepped forward, her hand reaching out to take the Staff of Wisdom. As she lifted it from the altar, the air around them shimmered with magic, and the runes on the staff glowed brightly.

"We've done it," Elara said, her voice filled with pride. "We've gathered all the relics."

With the Staff of Wisdom in their possession, the group felt a renewed sense of purpose. They had faced their final trial and emerged victorious, their bond stronger than ever.

The journey ahead would be long and difficult, but they were ready to face whatever challenges lay in their path. Together, they would confront the dark mage and save Eldoria from the encroaching darkness. The final confrontation awaited them, and they were determined to see it through to the end.

Chapter 6: The Enchanted Forest

Entering the Enchanted Forest

The group stood at the edge of the Enchanted Forest, its towering trees casting long shadows in the fading light. The air was thick with the scent of pine and earth, and a faint mist clung to the ground, giving the forest an otherworldly feel. The trees seemed to whisper secrets, their branches swaying gently in an unseen breeze.

"This is it," Eldrin said, his voice filled with awe. "The Enchanted Forest. A place of ancient magic and mystery."

Elara nodded, her heart pounding with anticipation. "We need to be prepared. The forest is known for its illusions and enchantments. It will test our resolve."

Kael drew his sword, his eyes scanning the dense foliage. "Let's stick together and watch each other's backs."

They stepped into the forest, the air growing cooler and the light dimmer as they moved deeper inside. The trees closed in around them, their branches intertwining to form a canopy that blocked out the sun. The ground was covered in a thick carpet of moss, and the air was filled with the sound of rustling leaves and distant bird calls.

As they ventured further, the forest began to play on their fears and insecurities. Shadows flickered at the edge of their vision, and strange whispers filled the air. The path seemed to twist and turn, leading them in circles and making it difficult to find their way.

"This place is messing with our minds," Lyra muttered, her eyes darting around nervously. "We need to stay focused."

Aeliana, her eyes glowing softly in the dim light, nodded. "The forest is testing us. We must rely on each other and trust in our bond."

The group pressed on, their steps cautious and deliberate. The forest seemed to shift around them, creating illusions and obstacles that tested their resolve. At one point, they came upon a clearing filled with beautiful, glowing flowers. The flowers emitted a sweet, intoxicating scent that made them feel drowsy and disoriented.

"We can't stay here," Kael said, shaking his head to clear the fog. "It's a trap."

Elara nodded, her mind racing. "We need to keep moving. Aeliana, can you guide us?"

Aeliana closed her eyes, her magic weaving through the air like a gentle breeze. "Follow me," she said, her voice calm and steady. "I can sense the true path."

They followed Aeliana through the forest, her presence a beacon of light in the darkness. The illusions and enchantments continued to test them, but they relied on each other and their trust in Aeliana to stay on the right path.

As they moved deeper into the forest, the air grew colder and the light dimmer. The trees seemed to close in around them, their branches reaching out like skeletal fingers. The ground was uneven and covered in roots and rocks, making each step a challenge.

"This place is relentless," Thorne muttered, his breath coming in short gasps. "It's like the forest itself is trying to stop us."

Eldrin, his face lined with determination, used his magic to create a protective barrier against the forest's enchantments. "We must push through. The heart of the forest is within our reach."

The group pressed on, their resolve unwavering. The forest continued to test them, but they faced each challenge with determination and unity. They encountered illusions that played on their deepest fears, but they supported each other and refused to give in to the darkness.

Finally, they reached a clearing where the trees parted to reveal a path bathed in soft, golden light. The air was filled with the scent of blooming flowers, and the ground was covered in a thick carpet of moss.

"We did it," Elara said, her voice filled with relief. "We made it through the forest."

Kael nodded, his expression serious. "But the challenges are far from over. We need to stay vigilant."

With Aeliana's guidance and their trust in each other, the group had navigated the Enchanted Forest and emerged stronger for it. The journey ahead would be long and difficult, but they were ready to face whatever challenges lay in their path. Together, they would find the relics and save Eldoria from the encroaching darkness.

The Forest Guardian

The group moved deeper into the Enchanted Forest, the air growing cooler and the light dimmer with each step. The trees seemed to close in around them, their branches intertwining to form a dense canopy that blocked out the sun. The ground was covered in a thick carpet of moss, and the air was filled with the sound of rustling leaves and distant bird calls.

As they ventured further, the forest's magic became more palpable. The air shimmered with an ethereal glow, and the trees seemed to whisper secrets in a language only they could understand. The path twisted and turned, leading them deeper into the heart of the forest.

"We're getting close," Aeliana said, her eyes glowing softly in the dim light. "The guardian of this forest is near."

Elara nodded, her heart pounding with anticipation. "We need to be prepared. The guardian will test our intentions and our worthiness."

They continued along the path until they reached a clearing. In the center stood a massive tree, its branches reaching towards the sky. The tree radiated a powerful, ancient magic, and Elara knew they had found the heart of the forest.

Suddenly, the air around them shimmered, and a figure appeared before them. The guardian of the forest was a tall, graceful being, her hair flowing like liquid silver, her eyes glowing with an inner light. She wore a gown of leaves and flowers, and her presence seemed to make the very air shimmer.

"Welcome, travelers," she said, her voice like the rustle of leaves. "I am Sylphara, guardian of this forest. You seek passage through my domain, but first, you must prove your worthiness."

Elara stepped forward, her head bowed in respect. "We are ready to face your trial, Sylphara."

Sylphara's eyes scanned the group, her expression thoughtful. "Each of you must demonstrate your courage, wisdom, and compassion. Only then will you be deemed worthy of passage."

With a wave of her hand, the clearing transformed, and each member of the group found themselves facing a personal trial.

Elara stood in a darkened forest, the trees closing in around her. She could hear the whispers of the shadows, taunting her, trying to break her resolve. She took a deep breath, centering herself, and called upon her magic. A beam of light shot from her staff, dispelling the shadows and revealing a path forward.

Kael found himself on a battlefield, surrounded by enemies. His sword felt heavy in his hand, and doubt gnawed at his mind. But he remembered his training, his purpose, and fought with renewed strength. Each swing of his sword was precise and powerful, and he emerged victorious.

Lyra stood in a maze of mirrors, each reflection showing a different version of herself. She felt lost, unsure of who she truly was. But she remembered her skills, her quick wit, and used her daggers to shatter the mirrors, revealing the true path.

Eldrin faced a vision of his past, the mistakes he had made, the people he had lost. The weight of his years pressed down on him, but he remembered the wisdom he had gained, the knowledge he could share. He embraced his past, and the vision faded.

Thorne stood at the edge of a cliff, the wind howling around him. He felt the pull of the void, the temptation to give in to despair. But he remembered his duty, his strength, and took a step forward, finding solid ground beneath his feet.

When the trials were over, they found themselves back in the clearing, Sylphara standing before them. She smiled, her eyes filled with approval.

"You have proven your worthiness," she said. "Your courage, wisdom, and compassion have earned you passage through my forest."

She raised her hand, and a path appeared before them, bathed in soft, golden light. The air was filled with the scent of blooming flowers, and the ground was covered in a thick carpet of moss.

"Thank you, Sylphara," Elara said, her voice filled with gratitude. "We will honor your trust and continue our quest to save Eldoria."

With Sylphara's blessing, the group felt a renewed sense of purpose. They had faced their deepest fears and emerged stronger for it. The journey ahead would be long and difficult, but they were ready to face whatever challenges lay in their path. Together, they would find the relics and save Eldoria from the encroaching darkness.

The Hidden Village

The group continued their journey through the Enchanted Forest, the air growing warmer and the light brighter as they moved deeper into the heart of the ancient woods. The trees seemed to part before them, guiding their way with a gentle, almost sentient touch. The path was lined with vibrant flowers and lush greenery, the forest alive with the sounds of birdsong and rustling leaves.

As they walked, Elara felt a sense of peace settle over her. The trials they had faced had strengthened their bond, and she felt more confident than ever in their ability to succeed. But she knew that the forest still held many secrets, and they would need to remain vigilant.

After several hours of walking, they came upon a hidden village nestled within a secluded glade. The village was unlike anything they had ever seen, its houses built into the trunks of ancient trees and connected by winding bridges and pathways. The air was filled with the scent of blooming flowers and the soft hum of magic.

"This place is incredible," Lyra whispered, her eyes wide with wonder. "I've never seen anything like it."

Eldrin nodded, his expression serious. "This village is home to a reclusive tribe of magical beings. They are wary of outsiders and protective of their secrets. We must tread carefully."

As they entered the village, they were met with curious glances and wary stares from the villagers. The inhabitants were a mix of fae, elves, and other magical beings, their eyes filled with a mixture of curiosity and suspicion.

"We mean you no harm," Elara said, her voice calm and steady. "We are on a quest to save Eldoria from the encroaching darkness. We seek your guidance and assistance."

An elderly elf stepped forward, his eyes sharp and piercing. "You speak of the dark mage," he said, his voice filled with a mixture of fear and anger. "His influence has spread far and wide, even reaching our hidden village. Why should we trust you?"

Kael stepped forward, his hand resting on the hilt of his sword. "We have faced many challenges and proven our worthiness. We seek only to protect Eldoria and restore the balance of magic."

The elder studied them for a moment, his eyes narrowing. "Very well. You may stay, but you must prove your intentions. Our village has been plagued by dark creatures, and we need your help to drive them away."

Elara nodded, her heart swelling with determination. "We will do whatever it takes to earn your trust."

The group set to work, helping the villagers fortify their defenses and prepare for the impending attack. They worked tirelessly, their bond growing stronger with each passing hour. As night fell, the village was ready, its inhabitants standing side by side with their new allies.

The dark creatures attacked under the cover of darkness, their eyes glowing with a malevolent light. The air was filled with the sounds of battle, the clash of metal and the crackle of magic. The group fought with everything they had, their skills and teamwork tested to the limit.

Kael's sword flashed in the dim light, each strike precise and powerful. Lyra moved with her usual grace and agility, her daggers finding their mark with deadly accuracy. Eldrin used his magic to create protective barriers, shielding the villagers from the worst of the attacks. Thorne's arrows flew true, each one finding its mark with deadly precision. Aeliana summoned vines from the ground, entangling the creatures and holding them in place.

Elara raised her staff, chanting a powerful incantation. A beam of light shot from her staff, striking the dark creatures and enveloping them in a shimmering aura. The creatures cried out in pain, their bodies writhing as the light purified the darkness within them.

As the last of the creatures fell, the village fell silent once more. The villagers stood in awe, their eyes filled with gratitude and respect.

"You have proven your worthiness," the elder said, his voice filled with admiration. "You have earned our trust and our assistance."

Elara smiled, her heart swelling with pride. "Thank you. We are honored to have your support."

The villagers shared their knowledge of the forest and the dark mage, providing valuable information that would aid the group in their quest. They learned of hidden paths and secret places, and the villagers offered their magic to help protect and guide them.

As they prepared to leave the village, Elara felt a renewed sense of purpose. They had gained valuable allies and strengthened their bond as a team. The journey ahead would be long and difficult, but they were ready to face whatever challenges lay in their path. Together, they would find the relics and save Eldoria from the encroaching darkness.

The Enchanted River

The group left the hidden village with the villagers' blessings and valuable information about the forest and the dark mage. They moved deeper into the Enchanted Forest, the air growing warmer and the light brighter as they followed a winding path. The trees seemed to part before them, guiding their way with a gentle, almost sentient touch.

After several hours of walking, they reached a mystical river that flowed through the heart of the forest. The water was crystal clear, shimmering with an ethereal glow. The river's banks were lined with vibrant flowers and lush greenery, and the air was filled with the sound of rushing water and the sweet scent of blooming flowers.

"This is the Enchanted River," Eldrin said, his voice filled with awe. "Its waters are imbued with powerful magic. We must find a way to cross it."

Elara nodded, her heart pounding with anticipation. "We need to be careful. The river is guarded by magical creatures and enchanted currents."

Kael drew his sword, his eyes scanning the riverbank. "Let's stick together and watch each other's backs."

As they approached the river, they could feel the magic thrumming in the air. The water seemed to dance and shimmer, creating illusions and obstacles that threatened to separate them. The river's magic tested their resolve and unity, creating challenges that pushed them to their limits.

At one point, they encountered a series of stepping stones that led across the river. The stones were spaced unevenly, and the water between them was filled with swirling currents and hidden dangers.

"We need to be careful," Lyra said, her eyes narrowing as she studied the stones. "One wrong step, and we'll be swept away."

Aeliana, her eyes glowing softly in the dim light, nodded. "The river's magic is strong. We must use our combined skills to cross safely."

Kael took the lead, his strong arms and steady balance allowing him to navigate the stepping stones with ease. Elara followed, her staff glowing softly to light her way. Lyra moved with her usual grace and agility, her quick reflexes serving her well. Eldrin used his magic to create protective barriers, shielding the group from the worst of the river's enchantments. Thorne's knowledge of the forest and his keen senses guided them through the most treacherous sections of the path.

As they reached the middle of the river, the water began to churn and swirl, creating powerful currents that threatened to pull them under. The air was filled with the sound of rushing water and the roar of the river's magic.

"We need to stay together," Kael shouted over the noise. "Hold on to each other and keep moving."

The group linked hands, their bond and determination giving them the strength to push through the river's challenges. They moved carefully, their steps deliberate and coordinated. The river's magic continued to test them, creating illusions and obstacles that threatened to separate them, but they relied on each other and their trust in their bond to stay on the right path.

At one point, a massive water serpent emerged from the depths of the river, its eyes glowing with a malevolent light. The serpent lunged at them, its powerful jaws snapping and its body coiling around the stepping stones.

Kael raised his sword, his eyes filled with determination. "We need to fight it off. Stay together and protect each other."

Elara raised her staff, chanting a powerful incantation. A beam of light shot from her staff, striking the serpent and enveloping it in a shimmering aura. The serpent roared in pain, its body writhing as the light purified the darkness within it.

Lyra moved with her usual grace and agility, her daggers finding their mark with deadly accuracy. Eldrin used his magic to create protective barriers, shielding the group from the serpent's attacks. Thorne's arrows flew true, each one finding its mark with deadly precision. Aeliana summoned vines from the riverbank, entangling the serpent and holding it in place.

With a final, powerful strike, Kael drove his sword into the serpent's heart. The creature let out an agonized roar before collapsing into the water, its body dissolving into mist.

"We did it," Elara said, her voice filled with relief. "But we need to keep moving. The river's magic is still strong."

The group continued their journey across the river, their bond and determination giving them the strength to push through the challenges. They moved carefully, their steps deliberate and coordinated, relying on each other and their trust in their bond to stay on the right path.

Finally, they reached the other side of the river, the air filled with the sweet scent of blooming flowers and the soft hum of magic. The group stood on the riverbank, their hearts filled with relief and pride.

"We made it," Kael said, his voice filled with determination. "But the challenges are far from over. We need to stay vigilant."

With the Enchanted River behind them, the group felt a renewed sense of purpose. They had faced the river's magic and emerged stronger for it. The journey ahead would be long and difficult, but they were ready to face whatever challenges lay in their path. Together, they would find the relics and save Eldoria from the encroaching darkness.

The Heart of the Forest

The group stood on the riverbank, their hearts filled with relief and pride after crossing the Enchanted River. The air was thick with the scent of blooming flowers and the soft hum of magic. They knew the journey ahead would be challenging, but they were ready to face whatever lay in their path.

"We're close," Eldrin said, his voice filled with determination. "The heart of the forest is just ahead."

Elara nodded, her heart pounding with anticipation. "We need to be prepared. The dark mage's influence is strong here."

They moved deeper into the forest, the trees parting before them to reveal a path bathed in soft, golden light. The air grew warmer, and the light brighter as they approached the heart of the Enchanted Forest. The ground was covered in a thick carpet of moss, and the air was filled with the sound of rustling leaves and distant bird calls.

As they reached the heart of the forest, they were met with a breathtaking sight. The clearing was filled with ancient trees, their branches intertwined to form a canopy that shimmered with an ethereal glow. In the center of the clearing stood a massive tree, its trunk covered in intricate runes and symbols. The tree radiated a powerful, ancient magic, and Elara knew they had found the heart of the forest.

"This is it," Aeliana said, her eyes glowing with a soft, inner light. "The heart of the Enchanted Forest. A place of immense power and beauty."

But as they approached the tree, they could feel the dark mage's influence beginning to corrupt the forest's magic. The air grew colder, and the light dimmer as shadows crept across the clearing. The ground trembled beneath their feet, and the trees seemed to shudder in response.

"We need to act quickly," Kael said, his hand resting on the hilt of his sword. "The dark mage's minions will be here soon."

As if on cue, the dark mage's minions emerged from the shadows, their eyes glowing with a malevolent light. The air was filled with the sound of snarling and growling, and the ground trembled beneath their feet.

"Get ready," Elara said, her voice steady. "We need to protect the heart of the forest and purify its magic."

A fierce battle ensued, the air filled with the clash of metal and the crackle of magic. The dark mage's minions were swift and deadly, their attacks relentless. But the group fought back with equal determination, their bond stronger than ever.

Kael's sword flashed in the dim light, each strike precise and powerful. Lyra moved with her usual grace and agility, her daggers finding their mark with deadly accuracy. Eldrin used his magic to create protective barriers, shielding the group from the worst of the attacks. Thorne's arrows flew true, each one finding its mark with deadly precision. Aeliana summoned vines from the ground, entangling the minions and holding them in place.

Elara raised her staff, chanting a powerful incantation. A beam of light shot from her staff, striking the dark mage's minions and enveloping them in a shimmering aura. The minions cried out in pain, their bodies writhing as the light purified the darkness within them.

The battle was fierce and chaotic, each member of the group facing their own personal struggles. Kael fought with a ferocity born of desperation, his attacks swift and deadly. Lyra moved with agility and grace, her quick reflexes saving her from countless dangers. Eldrin used his magic to create protective barriers, shielding the group from the worst of the attacks. Thorne's arrows flew true, each one finding its mark with deadly precision. Aeliana's presence was a calming force, her magic weaving through the air like a gentle breeze.

As the last of the dark mage's minions fell, the clearing fell silent once more. The group stood panting, their weapons at the ready, their eyes scanning the clearing for any remaining threats.

"We did it," Elara said, her voice filled with relief. "But we need to purify the heart of the forest."

Aeliana stepped forward, her eyes glowing with a soft, inner light. "I can help with that. The forest's magic is strong, but it needs our combined strength to overcome the corruption."

The group gathered around the massive tree, their hands joined in a circle. Aeliana began to chant a powerful incantation, her voice like the rustle of leaves. The air around them shimmered with magic, and the runes on the tree glowed brightly.

Elara raised her staff, adding her own magic to the incantation. Kael, Lyra, Eldrin, and Thorne followed suit, their combined magic weaving through the air like a tapestry of light.

The ground trembled beneath their feet, and the air was filled with the sound of rustling leaves and distant bird calls. The shadows began to recede, and the light grew brighter as the forest's magic was purified.

With a final, powerful surge of magic, the corruption was driven from the heart of the forest. The air was filled with the sweet scent of blooming flowers, and the ground was covered in a thick carpet of moss. The trees shimmered with an ethereal glow, their branches swaying gently in an unseen breeze.

"We did it," Elara said, her voice filled with pride. "We purified the heart of the forest."

Kael nodded, his expression serious. "But the final confrontation with the dark mage awaits us. We need to be ready."

With the heart of the forest purified and their bond stronger than ever, the group felt a renewed sense of purpose. They had faced the dark mage's minions and emerged victorious, their bond stronger than ever.

The journey ahead would be long and difficult, but they were ready to face whatever challenges lay in their path. Together, they would confront the dark mage and save Eldoria from the encroaching darkness. The final confrontation awaited them, and they were determined to see it through to the end.

Chapter 7: The Lost City

Arrival at the Lost City

The sun was setting as Elara, Kael, Lyra, Eldrin, Thorne, and Aeliana arrived at the outskirts of the Lost City. The ancient ruins loomed ahead, their crumbling walls and towering spires casting long shadows in the fading light. The air was thick with the scent of moss and decay, and a sense of foreboding hung over the group.

"This is it," Eldrin said, his voice filled with awe. "The Lost City. A place of ancient power and hidden dangers."

Elara nodded, her heart pounding with anticipation. "We need to be careful. The dark mage's influence is strong here."

Kael drew his sword, his eyes scanning the ruins for any signs of danger. "Let's stick together and watch each other's backs."

They stepped into the city, the air growing cooler and the light dimmer as they moved deeper inside. The streets were lined with the remnants of once-grand buildings, their walls covered in thick vines and their windows shattered. The ground was uneven and covered in debris, making each step a challenge.

As they explored the city, they encountered remnants of its former glory—statues of ancient heroes, fountains that had long since run dry, and murals depicting scenes of powerful magic. But they also saw signs of the dark mage's influence—symbols etched into the walls, dark creatures lurking in the shadows, and traps designed to deter intruders.

"We need to stay alert," Lyra said, her eyes darting around nervously. "The dark mage has left traps and obstacles to slow us down."

Eldrin nodded, his expression serious. "We must use our combined knowledge and skills to navigate these dangers."

At one point, they came upon a series of pressure plates embedded in the ground, each one inscribed with a different symbol. Eldrin knelt down, studying the symbols carefully.

"These symbols represent different elements," he said, his voice thoughtful. "We need to step on the plates in the correct order to deactivate the trap."

Kael raised an eyebrow. "And how do we know the correct order?"

Eldrin smiled, his eyes twinkling with excitement. "We use our knowledge and intuition. The elements must be balanced—fire, water, earth, and air."

They worked together, carefully stepping on the plates in the correct order. The trap deactivated with a soft click, and they moved forward, their confidence growing with each success. But the challenges grew more difficult as they progressed, testing their skills and teamwork.

As they ventured deeper into the city, they encountered more traps and obstacles—hidden pits, enchanted barriers, and dark creatures that attacked without warning. Each challenge pushed them to their limits, but they relied on each other and their combined strengths to overcome them.

At one point, they found themselves in a narrow alleyway, the walls closing in around them. The air was thick with the scent of decay, and the ground was covered in a thick layer of dust. As they moved forward, they heard a faint clicking sound, and the walls began to close in on them.

"We need to move quickly," Kael said, his voice filled with urgency. "The walls are closing in."

Elara raised her staff, chanting a quick incantation. A beam of light shot from her staff, striking the walls and slowing their movement. Lyra moved with her usual grace and agility, her quick reflexes allowing her to navigate the narrow space with ease. Eldrin used his magic to create a protective barrier, shielding the group from the worst of the pressure. Thorne's arrows flew true, each one finding its mark and disabling the mechanisms that controlled the walls.

With a final, powerful push, they made it through the alleyway and into a wide courtyard. The air was filled with the scent of blooming flowers, and the ground was covered in a thick carpet of moss. The courtyard was bathed in soft, golden light, and the group felt a sense of relief wash over them.

"We did it," Elara said, her voice filled with pride. "We made it through the traps."

Kael nodded, his expression serious. "But the challenges are far from over. We need to stay vigilant."

With their combined knowledge and skills, the group had navigated the dangers of the Lost City and emerged stronger for it. The journey ahead would be long and difficult, but they were ready to face whatever challenges lay in their path. Together, they would find the relics and save Eldoria from the encroaching darkness.

The Ancient Temple

The group stood in the wide courtyard, the soft, golden light casting a warm glow on their faces. The air was filled with the scent of blooming flowers, and the ground was covered in a thick carpet of moss. They had successfully navigated the traps and obstacles of the Lost City, but they knew their journey was far from over.

In the center of the courtyard stood the central temple, a massive structure that towered above the surrounding ruins. The temple's walls were covered in intricate carvings and ancient runes, and the air around it shimmered with powerful enchantments.

"This is it," Eldrin said, his voice filled with awe. "The central temple. The heart of the Lost City."

Elara nodded, her heart pounding with anticipation. "We need to be prepared. The temple is filled with ancient magic and powerful enchantments. It will test us in ways we can't imagine."

Kael drew his sword, his eyes scanning the temple's entrance. "Let's stick together and watch each other's backs."

They approached the temple, the air growing cooler and the light dimmer as they moved closer. The entrance was guarded by a series of magical barriers, each one shimmering with a different color. The barriers pulsed with energy, creating a formidable obstacle.

"We need to deactivate these barriers to gain entry," Eldrin said, his eyes scanning the runes. "Each barrier is tied to a different element—fire, water, earth, and air. We must solve the puzzles associated with each element to proceed."

The group split up, each member taking on a different element. Elara approached the barrier tied to fire, her staff glowing softly in the dim light. The puzzle before her was a series of symbols, each one representing a different aspect of fire. She studied the symbols carefully, her mind racing as she tried to decipher the correct sequence.

Kael took on the barrier tied to earth, his strong hands manipulating a series of levers and gears. The puzzle required him to balance the elements of earth, creating a stable foundation that would deactivate the barrier. His muscles strained with the effort, but he remained focused and determined.

Lyra approached the barrier tied to water, her quick reflexes and sharp mind serving her well. The puzzle was a series of interconnected pipes and valves, each one controlling the flow of water. She moved with agility and precision, her fingers dancing over the valves as she adjusted the flow.

Eldrin took on the barrier tied to air, his magic weaving through the air like a gentle breeze. The puzzle required him to manipulate the currents of air, creating a harmonious flow that would deactivate the barrier. His eyes glowed with concentration as he chanted a series of incantations, his magic resonating with the barrier's energy.

As they worked on their respective puzzles, the air around them shimmered with magic. The barriers pulsed with energy, creating a formidable obstacle that tested their intelligence, patience, and magical abilities. Tension rose within the group as they struggled to solve the puzzles, their frustrations and insecurities coming to the surface.

"This is impossible," Lyra muttered, her breath coming in short gasps. "We'll never get through these barriers."

Elara took a deep breath, trying to calm her racing thoughts. "We need to stay focused. We can do this if we work together."

Kael nodded, his expression serious. "Elara's right. We've faced tougher challenges before. We just need to keep pushing forward."

With renewed determination, the group continued to work on their puzzles. They relied on each other's strengths and supported one another through the difficult moments. Slowly but surely, the barriers began to weaken, their energy dissipating as the puzzles were solved.

Finally, with a soft click, the last barrier deactivated, and the entrance to the temple stood open before them. The air was filled with the scent of ancient magic, and the light inside the temple glowed with a soft, ethereal light.

"We did it," Elara said, her voice filled with pride. "We made it through the barriers."

Kael nodded, his expression serious. "But the challenges are far from over. We need to stay vigilant."

With their combined knowledge and skills, the group had successfully navigated the temple's defenses and gained entry to the inner sanctum. The journey ahead would be long and difficult, but they were ready to face whatever challenges lay in their path. Together, they would find the relics and save Eldoria from the encroaching darkness.

The Dark Mage's Ambush

The group stepped into the inner sanctum of the ancient temple, their hearts pounding with anticipation. The air was thick with the scent of old parchment and the faint hum of residual magic. The walls were lined with shelves filled with ancient tomes and artifacts, their surfaces covered in a fine layer of dust. The light inside the temple glowed with a soft, ethereal light, casting long shadows on the floor.

"This place is incredible," Lyra whispered, her eyes wide with wonder. "I've never seen anything like it."

Eldrin nodded, his expression serious. "The inner sanctum of the temple. This is where the most powerful relics and knowledge are kept."

As they moved deeper into the sanctum, they felt a growing sense of unease. The air grew colder, and the light dimmer as shadows crept across the room. The ground trembled beneath their feet, and the walls seemed to close in around them.

"We need to be careful," Kael said, his hand resting on the hilt of his sword. "The dark mage's influence is strong here."

Suddenly, a dark figure emerged from the shadows, his eyes glowing with a malevolent light. The air around him crackled with dark energy, and the ground trembled beneath his feet.

"Welcome, travelers," the dark mage said, his voice cold and menacing. "I've been expecting you."

The group turned to face the dark mage, their weapons at the ready. "Who are you?" Elara demanded, her voice steady despite the fear gnawing at her insides.

The dark mage stepped forward, his eyes scanning the group. "I am Malakar, the dark mage who will bring about the end of Eldoria. And you, my dear Elara, are the last obstacle in my path."

Elara's heart pounded in her chest, but she stood her ground. "We won't let you destroy Eldoria. We will stop you."

Malakar laughed, a cold, hollow sound. "You think you can stop me? You are nothing but pawns in a game you cannot hope to win."

He raised his hand, and the air around them shimmered with dark energy. The ground trembled, and the walls seemed to close in around them. The group felt a wave of fear and doubt wash over them, their insecurities and fears brought to the surface.

"You are weak," Malakar said, his voice filled with contempt. "You cannot hope to defeat me."

Kael stepped forward, his sword raised. "We are stronger than you think. We will fight for Eldoria and for each other."

A fierce battle ensued, the air filled with the clash of metal and the crackle of magic. Malakar's dark energy was powerful and relentless, his attacks swift and deadly. But the group fought back with equal determination, their bond stronger than ever.

Kael's sword flashed in the dim light, each strike precise and powerful. Lyra moved with her usual grace and agility, her daggers finding their mark with deadly accuracy. Eldrin used his magic to create protective barriers, shielding the group from the worst of Malakar's attacks. Thorne's arrows flew true, each one finding its mark with deadly precision. Aeliana summoned vines from the ground, entangling Malakar and holding him in place.

Elara raised her staff, chanting a powerful incantation. A beam of light shot from her staff, striking Malakar and enveloping him in a shimmering aura. Malakar roared in pain, his body writhing as the light purified the darkness within him.

"You cannot defeat me," Malakar snarled, his eyes filled with rage. "I will destroy you all."

Despite Malakar's efforts to turn them against each other, the group remained united. They fought with everything they had, their resolve and unity unwavering. They pushed Malakar back, their combined strength and determination driving him to the brink of defeat.

With a final, powerful strike, Kael drove his sword into Malakar's heart. The dark mage let out an agonized roar before collapsing to the ground, his body dissolving into mist.

"We did it," Elara said, her voice filled with relief. "But we need to be careful. Malakar may have escaped, but he will return."

Kael nodded, his expression serious. "We need to stay vigilant. The final confrontation with Malakar awaits us."

With Malakar driven back and their bond stronger than ever, the group felt a renewed sense of purpose. They had faced the dark mage and emerged victorious, but they knew the journey ahead would be long and difficult. Together, they would find the relics and save Eldoria from the encroaching darkness. The final confrontation awaited them, and they were determined to see it through to the end.

The Hidden Chamber

The air was thick with tension as the group stood in the aftermath of their battle with Malakar. The dark mage had been driven back, but the sense of foreboding lingered. The inner sanctum of the temple was filled with the soft glow of ancient magic, casting long shadows on the walls lined with shelves of ancient tomes and artifacts.

"We need to find out more about Malakar's plans," Elara said, her voice steady despite the lingering fear. "There must be something here that can help us."

Eldrin nodded, his eyes scanning the room. "The temple holds many secrets. We need to search carefully."

As they began to explore the inner sanctum, they discovered a hidden door concealed behind a tapestry depicting a scene of powerful magic. The door was covered in intricate runes, and the air around it shimmered with enchantments.

"This must be the hidden chamber," Lyra said, her eyes wide with curiosity. "Let's see what's inside."

Kael stepped forward, his hand resting on the hilt of his sword. "Be ready for anything. Malakar may have left traps."

Elara raised her staff, chanting a series of incantations to dispel the enchantments. The runes glowed brightly before fading away, and the door creaked open, revealing a narrow staircase leading down into the darkness.

The group descended the staircase, their footsteps echoing softly in the confined space. The air grew cooler and the light dimmer as they moved deeper into the hidden chamber. At the bottom of the stairs, they found themselves in a small room filled with ancient texts and artifacts.

"This is incredible," Eldrin said, his voice filled with awe. "These texts are centuries old. They may hold the key to understanding Malakar's plans."

They began to search the room, carefully examining the texts and artifacts. Elara's fingers brushed over the spines of ancient books, her eyes scanning the titles for anything that might provide a clue. Lyra moved with her usual grace and agility, her keen eyes spotting hidden compartments and secret passages.

As they delved deeper into their search, they uncovered a series of scrolls that detailed the history of the dark mage and his rise to power. The scrolls spoke of ancient rituals and forbidden magic, revealing the full extent of Malakar's ambitions.

"This is it," Eldrin said, his voice trembling with excitement. "These scrolls contain crucial information about Malakar's plans. He seeks to harness the power of the relics to open a portal to the Shadow Realm and unleash its dark forces upon Eldoria."

Kael's expression grew serious. "We need to stop him. If he succeeds, it will mean the end of our world."

Elara nodded, her heart pounding with determination. "We have to find the final relic and confront Malakar before it's too late."

As they continued to search the hidden chamber, they discovered a detailed map of the Lost City, marked with symbols and runes. The map revealed the location of the final relic, hidden deep within the heart of the city.

"This map is invaluable," Lyra said, her eyes scanning the intricate details. "It shows us the way to the final relic."

Thorne's expression was grim. "But it also shows us the full extent of Malakar's influence. The city is filled with his minions and traps. We need to be prepared for anything."

Aeliana's presence was a calming force, her eyes glowing softly in the dim light. "We have faced many challenges and emerged stronger for it. We will face this one together."

With their newfound knowledge and a renewed sense of purpose, the group felt a surge of determination. They had uncovered crucial information about Malakar's plans and the location of the final relic. The journey ahead would be long and difficult, but they were ready to face whatever challenges lay in their path.

"We need to prepare for the final confrontation," Elara said, her voice filled with resolve. "Malakar won't stop until he has the relics. We have to stop him."

Kael nodded, his expression serious. "Let's gather what we need and get out of here. The final battle awaits us."

With the hidden chamber's secrets revealed and their bond stronger than ever, the group felt a renewed sense of purpose. They had faced the dark mage and emerged victorious, but they knew the journey ahead would be long and difficult. Together, they would find the final relic and save Eldoria from the encroaching darkness. The final confrontation awaited them, and they were determined to see it through to the end.

Departure and Determination

The group emerged from the hidden chamber, their hearts heavy with the knowledge they had uncovered. The ancient texts and artifacts had revealed the full extent of Malakar's plans, and the map had shown them the way to the final relic. The air in the inner sanctum was thick with the scent of old parchment and the faint hum of residual magic, casting long shadows on the walls lined with shelves of ancient tomes.

"We have what we need," Elara said, her voice steady despite the weight of their discovery. "We know where the final relic is hidden, and we know what Malakar plans to do. We have to stop him."

Kael nodded, his expression serious. "Let's gather our things and get out of here. The final battle awaits us."

They moved quickly, gathering the most important texts and artifacts and securing them in their packs. The air was filled with a sense of urgency, and the light inside the temple glowed with a soft, ethereal light. The ground trembled beneath their feet, and the walls seemed to close in around them as they prepared to leave.

As they stepped out into the wide courtyard, the soft, golden light cast a warm glow on their faces. The air was filled with the scent of blooming flowers, and the ground was covered in a thick carpet of moss. They took a moment to catch their breath, their hearts pounding with anticipation.

"We've come a long way," Lyra said, her voice thoughtful as she stared into the distance. "But the hardest part is still ahead of us."

Thorne nodded, his eyes reflecting the firelight. "Malakar won't stop until he has the relics. We need to be ready for anything."

Aeliana's presence was a calming force, her eyes glowing softly in the darkness. "We have each other," she said, her voice like the rustle of leaves. "Together, we are strong."

Elara felt a surge of gratitude for her companions. Each of them brought unique skills and knowledge to the group, and together, they were a formidable team. "We've faced many challenges already," she said, her voice filled with determination. "And we'll face many more. But I believe in us. We can do this."

Eldrin smiled, his eyes filled with wisdom. "The prophecy speaks of the Last Enchanter and the allies who will stand by their side. We are those allies. And we will succeed."

As they sat around the campfire, they shared stories and strengthened their bonds. Kael spoke of his time as a warrior, fighting to protect his homeland. Lyra recounted tales of her adventures as a rogue thief, her quick wit and sharp reflexes saving her from countless dangers. Eldrin shared his wisdom and knowledge of ancient magic, while Thorne spoke of his time in the mountains, his skills as a ranger honed by years of survival.

Aeliana, her voice like a gentle breeze, told stories of the Enchanted Forest and the creatures that dwelled within. Her presence brought a sense of calm and serenity to the group, and Elara felt a deep connection to the guardian of the forest.

As the fire burned low, Elara looked around at her companions, her heart filled with hope. They had come a long way since leaving Eldenwood, and the journey ahead would be even more challenging. But with their combined strength and determination, she knew they could succeed.

"We should rest," Kael said, his voice gentle but firm. "We'll need all our strength for the journey ahead."

They settled down for the night, each taking turns to keep watch. Elara lay beneath the stars, her mind racing with thoughts of the prophecy and the challenges that awaited them. She knew the path would be fraught with danger, but she was ready to face it.

In the quiet of the night, Elara felt a sense of peace. The prophecy had brought them together, and together, they would fight to save Eldoria. She closed her eyes, letting the sounds of the forest lull her to sleep, her heart filled with hope and determination.

The dawn broke with a soft, golden light, casting a warm glow over the ruins of the Lost City. Elara and her companions packed up their camp and prepared to continue their journey, their spirits high and their resolve unwavering.

As they set off towards their next destination, Elara felt a surge of excitement and anticipation. The journey ahead would be long and difficult, but they were ready to face whatever challenges lay in their path. Together, they would find the final relic and save Eldoria from the encroaching darkness. The final confrontation awaited them, and they were determined to see it through to the end.

9

Chapter 8: Betrayal

The Suspicion

The dense forest was alive with the sounds of rustling leaves and distant bird calls as Elara, Kael, Lyra, Eldrin, Thorne, and Aeliana made their way through the thick underbrush. The air was cool and damp, the scent of pine and earth filling their lungs. Despite the beauty of their surroundings, a sense of unease hung over the group, casting a shadow on their journey.

Elara walked at the front of the group, her staff glowing softly to light their way. She couldn't shake the feeling that something was amiss. The atmosphere was tense, and she had noticed strange behavior from one of their companions. Thorne, who had once been a steadfast ally, seemed distant and distracted. He often lagged behind the group, his eyes darting around nervously as if he were expecting an attack at any moment.

"Thorne, are you alright?" Elara asked, her voice gentle but probing.

Thorne looked up, his eyes wide with surprise. "I'm fine," he replied quickly, his voice tight. "Just keeping an eye out for any threats."

Elara nodded, but her suspicions were not eased. She had seen Thorne whispering to himself when he thought no one was watching, and his hands often trembled when he thought he was alone. She couldn't help but wonder if he was hiding something.

As they continued through the forest, Elara's mind raced with possibilities. Could Thorne be under the influence of the dark mage? Was he planning to betray them? The thought sent a chill down her spine, but she knew she couldn't act on mere suspicion. She needed more evidence before she could confront him.

That night, they set up camp in a secluded clearing, the fire casting flickering shadows on the surrounding trees. The group sat around the fire, their faces illuminated by the warm glow. Elara watched Thorne closely, her eyes narrowing as she tried to read his expression.

"Elara, are you alright?" Kael asked, his voice filled with concern.

Elara forced a smile, nodding. "I'm fine. Just tired from the journey."

Kael nodded, but his eyes remained on her, his concern evident. Elara appreciated his support, but she knew she couldn't share her suspicions without more proof. She needed to be sure before she accused Thorne of betrayal.

As the night wore on, the group settled down to sleep, each taking turns to keep watch. Elara volunteered for the first watch, her eyes scanning the darkness for any signs of danger. She couldn't shake the feeling that something was wrong, and she knew she needed to stay vigilant.

Hours passed, and the forest remained quiet. Elara's eyes grew heavy, but she forced herself to stay awake. She couldn't afford to let her guard down, not when the safety of her friends was at stake.

Just as she was about to wake Kael for his turn, she heard a faint whispering coming from the edge of the clearing. Her heart pounded in her chest as she crept closer, her staff held tightly in her hand. She peered through the underbrush, her eyes widening as she saw Thorne standing alone, his back to the camp.

Thorne's voice was low and urgent, his words barely audible. "I can't do this anymore. They're starting to suspect. I need more time."

Elara's blood ran cold as she realized what she was hearing. Thorne was communicating with someone—someone who wasn't part of their group. She knew she needed to act, but she couldn't risk alerting Thorne to her presence. She needed to gather more evidence before she confronted him.

With a heavy heart, Elara retreated back to the camp, her mind racing with the implications of what she had heard. She knew she needed to be careful, but she also knew she couldn't let Thorne's betrayal go unchecked. She would keep a close watch on him, hoping to uncover the truth without causing unnecessary conflict.

As she settled down to sleep, Elara's mind was filled with questions. Who was Thorne communicating with? What were his true intentions? And how could she protect her friends from the threat that lurked within their own group?

The journey ahead would be fraught with danger, but Elara was determined to uncover the truth and protect those she cared about. Together, they would face whatever challenges lay in their path, even if it meant confronting the darkness within their own ranks.

The Revelation

The night was still and quiet, the only sounds the crackling of the campfire and the distant calls of nocturnal creatures. The group had set up camp in a secluded clearing, the fire casting flickering shadows on the surrounding trees. Elara lay awake, her mind racing with the suspicions that had been gnawing at her all day.

She couldn't shake the feeling that Thorne was hiding something. His strange behavior, the whispered conversations—everything pointed to a betrayal. But she needed proof before she could confront him. She needed to be sure.

As the fire burned low, Elara decided to take a walk around the perimeter of the camp. She moved quietly, her staff glowing softly to light her way. The forest was dark and foreboding, the trees looming like silent sentinels. She kept her senses sharp, listening for any signs of danger.

As she neared the edge of the clearing, she heard voices—low and urgent. She crept closer, her heart pounding in her chest. The voices grew clearer, and she recognized one of them as Thorne's.

"I can't keep doing this," Thorne was saying, his voice filled with desperation. "They're starting to suspect. I need more time."

Elara's blood ran cold as she realized what she was hearing. Thorne was communicating with someone—someone who wasn't part of their group. She strained to hear the other voice, but it was too faint to make out.

"You promised me power," Thorne continued, his voice trembling. "But I can't betray them. They're my friends."

Elara's heart ached at the words. She had trusted Thorne, and now he was admitting to betrayal. She knew she needed to act, but she couldn't risk alerting Thorne to her presence. She needed to gather the group and confront him together.

With a heavy heart, Elara retreated back to the camp, her mind racing with the implications of what she had heard. She knew she needed to be careful, but she also knew she couldn't let Thorne's betrayal go unchecked.

She woke Kael first, her hand gently shaking his shoulder. "Kael, wake up. We need to talk."

Kael's eyes snapped open, his hand instinctively reaching for his sword. "What's wrong?" he asked, his voice low and alert.

"It's Thorne," Elara whispered, her voice trembling. "I overheard him talking to someone. He's been communicating with the dark mage."

Kael's expression hardened, and he nodded. "Wake the others. We need to confront him."

Elara moved quickly, waking Lyra, Eldrin, and Aeliana. They gathered around the campfire, their faces filled with concern and determination.

"What's going on?" Lyra asked, her eyes narrowing.

Elara took a deep breath, steadying herself. "I overheard Thorne talking to someone. He's been communicating with the dark mage. We need to confront him and find out the truth."

The group exchanged worried glances, but they nodded in agreement. They knew they couldn't afford to let a betrayal go unchecked.

Kael stood, his sword at the ready. "Let's do this."

They approached Thorne's tent, their footsteps silent on the soft ground. Elara's heart pounded in her chest as she reached out to pull back the flap. Thorne was sitting inside, his head in his hands. He looked up, his eyes widening in surprise.

"What's going on?" he asked, his voice trembling.

Elara stepped forward, her voice steady. "We know you've been communicating with the dark mage, Thorne. We heard you."

Thorne's face paled, and he shook his head. "It's not what you think. I was forced into it. The dark mage threatened my family. I had no choice."

Kael's eyes narrowed, his grip tightening on his sword. "Why didn't you tell us? We could have helped you."

Thorne's eyes filled with tears, and he looked down at the ground. "I was scared. I didn't know who to trust."

Elara's heart ached at the sight of Thorne's anguish. She wanted to believe him, but she knew they couldn't take any chances. "We need to know the truth, Thorne. Are you with us or against us?"

Thorne looked up, his eyes filled with determination. "I'm with you. I swear it. I'll do whatever it takes to prove my loyalty."

The group exchanged glances, their expressions filled with uncertainty. They knew they couldn't afford to let their guard down, but they also knew they couldn't abandon Thorne without giving him a chance to prove himself.

Kael nodded slowly. "Alright, Thorne. We'll give you a chance to prove your loyalty. But know this—we'll be watching you closely."

Thorne nodded, his eyes filled with gratitude. "Thank you. I won't let you down."

With the confrontation behind them, the group felt a sense of relief, but the tension remained. They knew the journey ahead would be fraught with danger, but they were determined to face it together. They would uncover the truth and protect those they cared about, even if it meant confronting the darkness within their own ranks.

The Confrontation

The campfire crackled softly, casting eerie shadows on the surrounding trees as the group gathered around Thorne. The tension was palpable, the air thick with unspoken fears and doubts. Elara stood at the forefront, her staff glowing softly in the dim light. Kael, Lyra, Eldrin, and Aeliana formed a protective circle around Thorne, their expressions a mix of anger, confusion, and concern.

"Thorne," Elara began, her voice steady but filled with emotion, "we need to know the truth. Why have you been communicating with the dark mage?"

Thorne's face was pale, his eyes wide with fear. He looked around at his friends, his gaze lingering on each of them before he spoke. "I didn't want to betray you," he said, his voice trembling. "The dark mage threatened my family. He said he would kill them if I didn't help him."

Kael's grip tightened on his sword, his knuckles white. "Why didn't you tell us? We could have helped you."

Thorne shook his head, tears streaming down his face. "I was scared. I didn't know who to trust. I thought if I could just buy some time, I could find a way to save my family without betraying you."

Lyra's eyes narrowed, her voice sharp. "And what exactly did you tell him? How much does he know about our plans?"

Thorne looked down at the ground, his shoulders shaking with silent sobs. "I told him about the relics. I told him where we were going. But I swear, I never meant to hurt any of you. I was trying to protect my family."

Eldrin stepped forward, his expression stern but compassionate. "Thorne, we understand the love you have for your family. But you put all of us in danger. We need to know if we can trust you."

Thorne looked up, his eyes filled with desperation. "Please, give me a chance to prove myself. I'll do whatever it takes. Just don't abandon me."

Elara's heart ached at the sight of Thorne's anguish. She wanted to believe him, but she knew they couldn't take any chances. "We need to decide what to do," she said, turning to the group. "Do we give Thorne a chance to prove his loyalty, or do we take more drastic measures?"

Kael's expression was hard, his voice cold. "We can't afford to let our guard down. If Thorne is truly loyal, he needs to prove it."

Lyra nodded, her eyes still wary. "Agreed. We can't risk the safety of the group."

Eldrin's voice was gentle but firm. "Thorne, if you want to prove your loyalty, you need to be willing to face the consequences of your actions. Are you prepared for that?"

Thorne nodded, his eyes filled with determination. "Yes. I'll do whatever it takes."

Aeliana stepped forward, her presence a calming force. "We will give you a chance, Thorne. But know this—we will be watching you closely. Any sign of betrayal, and you will face the consequences."

Thorne bowed his head, his voice barely above a whisper. "Thank you. I won't let you down."

With the confrontation behind them, the group felt a sense of relief, but the tension remained. They knew the journey ahead would be fraught with danger, and they couldn't afford to let their guard down. Thorne's betrayal had shaken their trust, but they were determined to face the challenges together.

As the night wore on, the group settled down to sleep, each taking turns to keep watch. Elara lay beneath the stars, her mind racing with thoughts of the confrontation and the challenges that awaited them. She knew the path would be difficult, but she was ready to face it.

In the quiet of the night, Elara felt a sense of resolve. They had confronted the darkness within their own ranks, and they would continue to fight for Eldoria. Together, they would face whatever challenges lay in their path, even if it meant confronting the darkness within themselves.

The Test of Loyalty

The morning sun filtered through the dense canopy of the forest, casting dappled shadows on the ground as the group prepared to continue their journey. The air was cool and crisp, filled with the scent of pine and earth. Despite the beauty of their surroundings, a sense of tension lingered over the camp. Thorne's betrayal had shaken their trust, and the atmosphere was thick with mistrust and unease.

Elara stood at the edge of the clearing, her eyes scanning the forest for any signs of danger. She couldn't shake the feeling that they were being watched, and she knew they needed to stay vigilant. Thorne's presence was a constant reminder of the dark mage's influence, and she couldn't afford to let her guard down.

"We need to keep moving," Kael said, his voice steady but filled with tension. "The dark mage won't wait for us to catch our breath."

Elara nodded, her heart heavy with the weight of their situation. "Agreed. But we also need to give Thorne a chance to prove his loyalty. We can't move forward with this cloud of mistrust hanging over us."

Lyra's eyes narrowed as she looked at Thorne. "And how do you propose we do that?"

Elara took a deep breath, her mind racing. "We give him a task. Something dangerous, but necessary. If he succeeds, it will show us that he's truly committed to our cause."

Kael's expression was hard, but he nodded. "Alright. What do you have in mind?"

Elara turned to Thorne, her eyes filled with determination. "There's a narrow pass up ahead, guarded by dark creatures. We need to clear the way if we're going to make it through. Thorne, I want you to take the lead on this. Show us that we can trust you."

Thorne's eyes widened, but he nodded, his jaw set with determination. "I'll do it. I won't let you down."

The group set off, the atmosphere still tense with mistrust. The path through the forest was narrow and winding, the trees closing in around them like silent sentinels. The air grew colder as they approached the pass, and the sound of distant growls and snarls filled the air.

As they reached the entrance to the pass, Thorne stepped forward, his bow at the ready. The pass was a narrow, rocky corridor, the walls towering high above them. The ground was uneven and covered in loose stones, making each step a challenge.

"We'll be right behind you," Kael said, his voice steady. "But this is your task, Thorne. Show us what you're made of."

Thorne nodded, his eyes filled with determination. He moved cautiously into the pass, his senses on high alert. The growls grew louder, and he could see the dark creatures lurking in the shadows, their eyes glowing with a malevolent light.

Thorne took a deep breath, his heart pounding in his chest. He drew an arrow from his quiver and nocked it, his hands steady despite the fear gnawing at his insides. He aimed carefully, his eyes narrowing as he focused on his target.

With a swift, precise movement, Thorne released the arrow. It flew through the air, striking one of the creatures in the heart. The creature let out a pained roar before collapsing to the ground, its body dissolving into mist.

The other creatures snarled and lunged at Thorne, their movements swift and deadly. Thorne moved with agility and precision, his arrows finding their mark with deadly accuracy. He fought with everything he had, his determination and resolve driving him forward.

The group watched from the entrance to the pass, their hearts pounding with a mix of fear and hope. Kael's grip tightened on his sword, ready to intervene if necessary. Lyra's eyes were fixed on Thorne, her expression a mix of suspicion and admiration.

As the last of the creatures fell, the pass fell silent once more. Thorne stood panting, his bow still at the ready. He looked back at the group, his eyes filled with a mixture of relief and determination.

"I did it," Thorne said, his voice trembling with emotion. "I cleared the way."

Elara stepped forward, her heart swelling with pride. "You did well, Thorne. You've shown us that we can trust you."

Kael nodded, his expression softening. "You've earned a second chance. But know this—we'll be watching you closely."

Thorne nodded, his eyes filled with gratitude. "Thank you. I won't let you down."

With the pass cleared and Thorne's loyalty tentatively restored, the group felt a renewed sense of purpose. They had faced a difficult challenge and emerged stronger for it. The journey ahead would be long and difficult, but they were ready to face whatever challenges lay in their path. Together, they would find the relics and save Eldoria from the encroaching darkness.

The Aftermath

The group emerged from the narrow pass, the air growing warmer and the light brighter as they left the dark creatures behind. The forest opened up before them, revealing a small village nestled in the mountains. The village was a safe haven, a place where they could rest and regroup before continuing their journey.

As they approached the village, the villagers greeted them with warm smiles and open arms. The air was filled with the scent of blooming flowers and the sound of children playing. It was a stark contrast to the tension and danger they had faced in the forest.

"We can rest here for a while," Eldrin said, his voice filled with relief. "The villagers are friendly and will provide us with food and shelter."

Elara nodded, her heart swelling with gratitude. "We need this. We've been through a lot, and we need to regain our strength."

The group settled into the village, their spirits lifted by the warm hospitality of the villagers. They were given comfortable rooms and plenty of food, and for the first time in days, they felt a sense of peace.

As night fell, they gathered around a large bonfire in the center of the village. The flames danced and flickered, casting a warm glow on their faces. The villagers joined them, sharing stories and songs that filled the air with laughter and joy.

Elara sat beside Kael, her eyes reflecting the firelight. "We've come a long way," she said, her voice thoughtful. "But the hardest part is still ahead of us."

Kael nodded, his expression serious. "Malakar won't stop until he has the relics. We need to be ready for anything."

Lyra, sitting across from them, added, "And we need to stay united. Thorne's betrayal shook us, but we can't let it break us."

Thorne, who had been sitting quietly, looked up, his eyes filled with determination. "I know I have a lot to prove, but I won't let you down. I'll do whatever it takes to earn your trust."

Eldrin placed a reassuring hand on Thorne's shoulder. "We believe in you, Thorne. You've shown us that you're willing to fight for our cause."

Aeliana's presence was a calming force, her eyes glowing softly in the firelight. "We have faced many challenges and emerged stronger for it. Together, we are unstoppable."

As they sat around the bonfire, the group reflected on their journey so far. They had faced countless dangers and overcome seemingly insurmountable obstacles. Their bond had been tested, but it had not broken. They were stronger and more determined than ever.

"We've come this far because we believe in each other," Elara said, her voice filled with conviction. "And we will continue to fight for Eldoria. Together, we will find the relics and stop Malakar."

Kael raised his sword, the blade gleaming in the firelight. "For Eldoria," he said, his voice strong and unwavering.

The rest of the group followed suit, raising their weapons and voices in unison. "For Eldoria!"

The villagers joined in, their voices echoing through the mountains. The air was filled with a sense of unity and determination, a powerful reminder of what they were fighting for.

As the night wore on, the group shared stories and strengthened their bonds. Kael spoke of his time as a warrior, fighting to protect his homeland. Lyra recounted tales of her adventures as a rogue thief, her quick wit and sharp reflexes saving her from countless dangers. Eldrin shared his wisdom and knowledge of ancient magic, while Thorne spoke of his time in the mountains, his skills as a ranger honed by years of survival.

Aeliana, her voice like a gentle breeze, told stories of the Enchanted Forest and the creatures that dwelled within. Her presence brought a sense of calm and serenity to the group, and Elara felt a deep connection to the guardian of the forest.

As the fire burned low, Elara looked around at her companions, her heart filled with hope. They had come a long way since leaving Eldenwood, and the journey ahead would be even more challenging. But with their combined strength and determination, she knew they could succeed.

"We should rest," Kael said, his voice gentle but firm. "We'll need all our strength for the journey ahead."

They settled down for the night, each taking turns to keep watch. Elara lay beneath the stars, her mind racing with thoughts of the prophecy and the challenges that awaited them. She knew the path would be fraught with danger, but she was ready to face it.

In the quiet of the night, Elara felt a sense of peace. The prophecy had brought them together, and together, they would fight to save Eldoria. She closed her eyes, letting the sounds of the forest lull her to sleep, her heart filled with hope and determination.

The dawn broke with a soft, golden light, casting a warm glow over the village. Elara and her companions packed up their camp and prepared to continue their journey, their spirits high and their resolve unwavering.

As they set off towards their next destination, Elara felt a surge of excitement and anticipation. The journey ahead would be long and difficult, but they were ready to face whatever challenges lay in their path. Together, they would find the final relic and save Eldoria from the encroaching darkness. The final confrontation awaited them, and they were determined to see it through to the end.

Chapter 9: The Dark Fortress

Approaching the Fortress

The landscape around them grew increasingly desolate as Elara, Kael, Lyra, Eldrin, Thorne, and Aeliana made their way towards the dark fortress. The air was thick with the scent of decay, and the sky was dark with storm clouds that seemed to swirl ominously above. The once vibrant land of Eldoria now lay in ruins, a testament to the dark mage's growing power.

"We're getting close," Eldrin said, his voice barely audible over the howling wind. "The fortress is just beyond that ridge."

Elara nodded, her heart pounding with a mix of fear and determination. "We need to be careful. The dark mage will have defenses in place to stop us."

As they approached the ridge, they could see the outer defenses of the fortress—patrols of dark creatures and magical barriers that shimmered with a malevolent energy. The creatures moved with a predatory grace, their eyes glowing with a sinister light.

"We can't take them head-on," Kael said, his eyes scanning the defenses. "We need to find a way to bypass or neutralize them without alerting the dark mage."

Lyra's eyes narrowed as she studied the patrols. "We can use stealth to get past the creatures, but those magical barriers will be a problem."

Eldrin nodded, his expression serious. "I'll need to use my magic to dispel the barriers, but it will take time. We'll need to create a distraction to keep the creatures occupied."

Aeliana stepped forward, her eyes glowing softly. "I can use my magic to create an illusion, something to draw their attention away from us."

Elara smiled, her heart swelling with gratitude for her friends. "Let's do it. We need to move quickly and stay together."

They moved cautiously towards the ridge, their steps silent on the rocky ground. Aeliana raised her hands, her magic weaving through the air like a gentle breeze. An illusion of a group of intruders appeared on the far side of the fortress, drawing the attention of the dark creatures.

As the creatures moved towards the illusion, Eldrin began to chant a series of incantations, his hands glowing with a soft, blue light. The magical barriers shimmered and flickered, their energy dissipating as Eldrin's magic took hold.

"Now," Kael whispered, his voice urgent. "Let's move."

They slipped past the patrols and through the weakened barriers, their hearts pounding with adrenaline. The fortress loomed ahead, its dark walls towering above them like a sinister monolith. The air was thick with the scent of decay, and the ground trembled beneath their feet.

As they approached the fortress walls, they could see a narrow tunnel hidden behind a tangle of vines and debris. The entrance was barely visible, but it offered a way into the heart of the dark mage's domain.

"This is our way in," Lyra said, her eyes scanning the tunnel. "But it won't be easy. The tunnel is likely filled with traps and obstacles."

Kael nodded, his expression grim. "We'll need to be careful. One wrong move, and we'll alert the dark mage to our presence."

Elara took a deep breath, her heart pounding with determination. "We can do this. We just need to stay focused and work together."

They entered the tunnel, the air growing colder and the light dimmer as they moved deeper inside. The walls were lined with ancient runes and symbols, their surfaces covered in a thick layer of dust. The ground was uneven and covered in debris, making each step a challenge.

As they ventured further, they encountered a series of traps and obstacles—hidden pits, enchanted barriers, and dark creatures that lurked in the shadows. Each challenge tested their skills and teamwork, but they relied on each other and their combined strengths to overcome them.

At one point, they came upon a narrow passageway filled with a series of pressure plates embedded in the ground. Eldrin knelt down, studying the symbols carefully.

"These symbols represent different elements," he said, his voice thoughtful. "We need to step on the plates in the correct order to deactivate the trap."

Kael raised an eyebrow. "And how do we know the correct order?"

Eldrin smiled, his eyes twinkling with excitement. "We use our knowledge and intuition. The elements must be balanced—fire, water, earth, and air."

They worked together, carefully stepping on the plates in the correct order. The trap deactivated with a soft click, and they moved forward, their confidence growing with each success. But the challenges grew more difficult as they progressed, testing their resolve and unity.

Finally, they reached the end of the tunnel, the air filled with the scent of ancient magic. The tunnel opened up into a vast chamber, the heart of the dark fortress. The walls were lined with shelves filled with ancient tomes and artifacts, their surfaces covered in a fine layer of dust.

"We did it," Elara said, her voice filled with pride. "We made it through the defenses."

Kael nodded, his expression serious. "But the hardest part is still ahead of us. We need to stay vigilant."

With their combined knowledge and skills, the group had successfully infiltrated the outer perimeter of the dark fortress. The journey ahead would be long and difficult, but they were ready to face whatever challenges lay in their path. Together, they would confront the dark mage and save Eldoria from the encroaching darkness.

Entering the Fortress

The narrow tunnel stretched before them, its entrance hidden behind a tangle of vines and debris. The air inside was cold and damp, the walls lined with ancient runes that glowed faintly in the dim light. Elara, Kael, Lyra, Eldrin, Thorne, and Aeliana stood at the threshold, their hearts pounding with anticipation and fear.

"This is our way in," Lyra said, her voice barely above a whisper. "But we need to be careful. The tunnel is likely filled with traps and obstacles."

Kael nodded, his expression grim. "We'll need to stay alert and move quietly. One wrong move, and we'll alert the dark mage to our presence."

Elara took a deep breath, her heart heavy with the weight of their mission. "We can do this. We just need to stay focused and work together."

They entered the tunnel, the air growing colder and the light dimmer as they moved deeper inside. The walls were covered in intricate carvings and symbols, their surfaces slick with moisture. The ground was uneven and littered with debris, making each step a challenge.

As they ventured further, they encountered the first of many traps—a series of pressure plates embedded in the ground. Eldrin knelt down, studying the symbols carefully.

"These symbols represent different elements," he said, his voice thoughtful. "We need to step on the plates in the correct order to deactivate the trap."

Kael raised an eyebrow. "And how do we know the correct order?"

Eldrin smiled, his eyes twinkling with excitement. "We use our knowledge and intuition. The elements must be balanced—fire, water, earth, and air."

They worked together, carefully stepping on the plates in the correct order. The trap deactivated with a soft click, and they moved forward, their confidence growing with each success. But the challenges grew more difficult as they progressed, testing their skills and teamwork.

At one point, they came upon a narrow passageway filled with a series of swinging blades. The blades moved with deadly precision, their edges gleaming in the dim light.

"We need to time our movements perfectly," Kael said, his eyes narrowing as he studied the blades. "One misstep, and we're done for."

Lyra moved with her usual grace and agility, her quick reflexes allowing her to navigate the passage with ease. She reached the other side and signaled for the others to follow. Kael went next, his strong arms and steady balance serving him well. Elara followed, her heart pounding as she timed her movements carefully. Eldrin used his magic to create a protective barrier, shielding himself from the worst of the blades. Thorne and Aeliana brought up the rear, their combined skills allowing them to navigate the passage safely.

As they reached the end of the passage, they found themselves in a small chamber filled with ancient artifacts and scrolls. The air was thick with the scent of old parchment and the faint hum of residual magic.

"This place is incredible," Lyra whispered, her eyes wide with wonder. "I've never seen anything like it."

Eldrin nodded, his expression serious. "These artifacts are centuries old. They may hold the key to understanding the dark mage's plans."

They began to search the chamber, carefully examining the artifacts and scrolls. Elara's fingers brushed over the spines of ancient books, her eyes scanning the titles for anything that might provide a clue. Lyra moved with her usual grace and agility, her keen eyes spotting hidden compartments and secret passages.

As they delved deeper into their search, they uncovered a series of scrolls that detailed the history of the dark mage and his rise to power. The scrolls spoke of ancient rituals and forbidden magic, revealing the full extent of Malakar's ambitions.

"This is it," Eldrin said, his voice trembling with excitement. "These scrolls contain crucial information about Malakar's plans. He seeks to harness the power of the relics to open a portal to the Shadow Realm and unleash its dark forces upon Eldoria."

Kael's expression grew serious. "We need to stop him. If he succeeds, it will mean the end of our world."

Elara nodded, her heart pounding with determination. "We have to find the final relic and confront Malakar before it's too late."

With their newfound knowledge and a renewed sense of purpose, the group felt a surge of determination. They had uncovered crucial information about Malakar's plans and the location of the final relic. The journey ahead would be long and difficult, but they were ready to face whatever challenges lay in their path.

"We need to keep moving," Kael said, his voice filled with resolve. "The final battle awaits us."

They left the chamber and continued through the tunnel, their hearts heavy with the weight of their mission. The air grew colder and the light dimmer as they moved deeper into the fortress. The walls were lined with ancient runes and symbols, their surfaces covered in a thick layer of dust.

As they reached the end of the tunnel, they found themselves in a vast chamber, the heart of the dark fortress. The walls were lined with shelves filled with ancient tomes and artifacts, their surfaces covered in a fine layer of dust.

"We did it," Elara said, her voice filled with pride. "We made it through the defenses."

Kael nodded, his expression serious. "But the hardest part is still ahead of us. We need to stay vigilant."

With their combined knowledge and skills, the group had successfully navigated the treacherous passage and entered the fortress undetected. The journey ahead would be long and difficult, but they were ready to face whatever challenges lay in their path. Together, they would confront the dark mage and save Eldoria from the encroaching darkness.

The Inner Sanctum

The vast chamber at the heart of the dark fortress was a place of shadows and whispers, its walls lined with ancient tomes and artifacts that seemed to pulse with a malevolent energy. The air was thick with the scent of decay and the faint hum of dark magic. Elara, Kael, Lyra, Eldrin, Thorne, and Aeliana stood at the entrance, their hearts pounding with a mix of fear and determination.

"This is it," Eldrin said, his voice barely above a whisper. "The inner sanctum of the dark fortress."

Elara nodded, her heart heavy with the weight of their mission. "We need to be prepared. The dark mage's most powerful minions will be guarding this place."

Kael drew his sword, his eyes scanning the chamber for any signs of danger. "Let's stick together and watch each other's backs."

As they stepped into the chamber, the air grew colder and the light dimmer. Shadows flickered at the edge of their vision, and the ground trembled beneath their feet. The walls seemed to close in around them, the dark magic pressing down on their spirits.

Suddenly, a group of dark creatures emerged from the shadows, their eyes glowing with a sinister light. They moved with a predatory grace, their claws and fangs gleaming in the dim light.

"Get ready," Kael said, his voice steady. "Here they come."

A fierce battle ensued, the air filled with the clash of metal and the crackle of magic. The dark creatures were swift and deadly, their attacks relentless. But the group fought back with equal determination, their bond stronger than ever.

Kael's sword flashed in the dim light, each strike precise and powerful. Lyra moved with her usual grace and agility, her daggers finding their mark with deadly accuracy. Eldrin used his magic to create protective barriers, shielding the group from the worst of the attacks. Thorne's arrows flew true, each one finding its mark and disabling the creatures. Aeliana summoned vines from the ground, entangling the creatures and holding them in place.

Elara raised her staff, chanting a powerful incantation. A beam of light shot from her staff, striking the dark creatures and enveloping them in a shimmering aura. The creatures roared in pain, their bodies writhing as the light purified the darkness within them.

"We need to keep moving," Kael shouted over the noise of the battle. "We can't let them overwhelm us."

The group pressed forward, their resolve and unity unwavering. They fought with everything they had, their skills and teamwork tested to the limit. The dark creatures were powerful, but the group's determination and strength proved to be greater.

As the last of the creatures fell, the chamber fell silent once more. The group stood panting, their weapons at the ready, their eyes scanning the room for any remaining threats.

"We did it," Elara said, her voice filled with relief. "But we need to stay vigilant. The dark mage will know we're here."

Kael nodded, his expression serious. "We need to find the dark mage's throne room. That's where the final confrontation will take place."

They moved cautiously through the chamber, their eyes scanning the shadows for any signs of danger. The air was thick with the scent of decay and the faint hum of dark magic. The walls were lined with shelves filled with ancient tomes and artifacts, their surfaces covered in a fine layer of dust.

As they reached the far end of the chamber, they found a massive door covered in intricate runes and symbols. The air around the door shimmered with a dark energy, and the ground trembled beneath their feet.

"This must be it," Eldrin said, his voice filled with awe. "The entrance to the dark mage's throne room."

Elara took a deep breath, her heart pounding with anticipation. "We need to be prepared. The dark mage will be waiting for us."

Kael raised his sword, his eyes filled with determination. "Let's do this. For Eldoria."

With their combined knowledge and skills, the group had successfully defeated the dark creatures and reached the entrance to the dark mage's throne room. The journey ahead would be long and difficult, but they were ready to face whatever challenges lay in their path. Together, they would confront the dark mage and save Eldoria from the encroaching darkness. The final confrontation awaited them, and they were determined to see it through to the end.

The Final Confrontation

The massive door to the dark mage's throne room loomed before them, its surface covered in intricate runes and symbols that pulsed with dark energy. The air around the door shimmered with a malevolent aura, and the ground trembled beneath their feet. Elara, Kael, Lyra, Eldrin,

Thorne, and Aeliana stood at the threshold, their hearts pounding with a mix of fear and determination.

"This is it," Eldrin said, his voice filled with awe. "The dark mage's throne room."

Elara nodded, her heart heavy with the weight of their mission. "We need to be prepared. Malakar will be waiting for us."

Kael raised his sword, his eyes filled with resolve. "Let's do this. For Eldoria."

With a deep breath, Elara raised her staff and chanted a series of incantations. The runes on the door glowed brightly before fading away, and the door creaked open, revealing a grand and ominous chamber filled with dark energy. The air inside was thick with the scent of decay and the faint hum of dark magic.

As they stepped into the throne room, they were met with a sight that sent chills down their spines. The chamber was vast, its walls lined with dark tapestries and ancient artifacts. At the far end of the room, seated on a throne of black stone, was Malakar, the dark mage. His eyes glowed with a sinister light, and the air around him crackled with dark energy.

"Welcome, travelers," Malakar said, his voice cold and menacing. "I've been expecting you."

The group stood their ground, their weapons at the ready. "Your reign of terror ends here, Malakar," Elara said, her voice steady despite the fear gnawing at her insides.

Malakar laughed, a cold, hollow sound that echoed through the chamber. "You think you can defeat me? You are nothing but pawns in a game you cannot hope to win."

He raised his hand, and the air around them shimmered with dark energy. The ground trembled, and the walls seemed to close in around them. The group felt a wave of fear and doubt wash over them, their insecurities and fears brought to the surface.

"You are weak," Malakar said, his voice filled with contempt. "You cannot hope to defeat me."

Kael stepped forward, his sword raised. "We are stronger than you think. We will fight for Eldoria and for each other."

A fierce battle ensued, the air filled with the clash of metal and the crackle of magic. Malakar's dark energy was powerful and relentless, his attacks swift and deadly. But the group fought back with equal determination, their bond stronger than ever.

Kael's sword flashed in the dim light, each strike precise and powerful. Lyra moved with her usual grace and agility, her daggers finding their mark with deadly accuracy. Eldrin used his magic to create protective barriers, shielding the group from the worst of Malakar's attacks. Thorne's arrows flew true, each one finding its mark and weakening the dark mage's defenses. Aeliana summoned vines from the ground, entangling Malakar and holding him in place.

Elara raised her staff, chanting a powerful incantation. A beam of light shot from her staff, striking Malakar and enveloping him in a shimmering aura. Malakar roared in pain, his body writhing as the light purified the darkness within him.

"You cannot defeat me," Malakar snarled, his eyes filled with rage. "I will destroy you all."

Despite Malakar's efforts to break their spirit and turn them against each other, the group remained united. They fought with everything they had, their resolve and unity unwavering. They pushed Malakar back, their combined strength and determination driving him to the brink of defeat.

With a final, powerful strike, Kael drove his sword into Malakar's heart. The dark mage let out an agonized roar before collapsing to the ground, his body dissolving into mist.

"We did it," Elara said, her voice filled with relief. "But we need to be careful. Malakar may have been defeated, but his influence is still strong."

Kael nodded, his expression serious. "We need to ensure the safety of the relics and each other. The fortress is still dangerous."

With Malakar defeated and their bond stronger than ever, the group felt a renewed sense of purpose. They had faced the dark mage and emerged victorious, but they knew the journey ahead would be long and difficult. Together, they would protect the relics and save Eldoria from the encroaching darkness. The final confrontation had tested their resolve, but they were determined to see their mission through to the end.

The Aftermath

The dark mage's throne room was eerily silent, the air still thick with the remnants of dark magic. Malakar's body had dissolved into mist, leaving behind only the faint echo of his malevolent presence. Elara, Kael, Lyra, Eldrin,

Thorne, and Aeliana stood in the center of the chamber, their hearts pounding with a mix of relief and exhaustion.

"We did it," Elara said, her voice trembling with emotion. "Malakar is defeated."

Kael nodded, his expression serious. "But we can't let our guard down. The fortress is still dangerous, and we need to get out of here."

As if on cue, the ground beneath their feet began to tremble, and the walls of the fortress shuddered. The dark magic that had held the structure together was unraveling, and the fortress was beginning to collapse.

"We need to move, now!" Kael shouted, his voice cutting through the growing chaos.

The group sprang into action, their movements swift and coordinated. They raced through the crumbling corridors, the ground shaking beneath their feet and debris falling around them. The air was filled with the sound of cracking stone and the roar of collapsing walls.

Elara led the way, her staff glowing brightly to light their path. She could feel the fortress's defenses activating in a final attempt to trap them, but she was determined to get her friends to safety.

As they reached the entrance to the tunnel, a massive stone block fell from the ceiling, blocking their path. "We need to find another way out!" Lyra shouted, her eyes scanning the collapsing structure.

Eldrin raised his hands, chanting a series of incantations. The stone block shimmered and began to dissolve, creating a narrow passageway. "This way!" he called, his voice filled with urgency.

They squeezed through the passageway, the ground trembling beneath their feet. The tunnel was filled with dust and debris, making it difficult to see and breathe. But they pressed on, their determination driving them forward.

As they neared the end of the tunnel, they could see the faint glow of daylight. "We're almost there!" Thorne shouted, his voice filled with hope.

But just as they were about to reach the exit, a series of dark creatures emerged from the shadows, their eyes glowing with a malevolent light. "We need to fight our way through!" Kael shouted, his sword flashing in the dim light.

A fierce battle ensued, the air filled with the clash of metal and the crackle of magic. The dark creatures were relentless, their attacks swift and deadly. But the group fought back with equal determination, their bond stronger than ever.

Kael's sword flashed in the dim light, each strike precise and powerful. Lyra moved with her usual grace and agility, her daggers finding their mark with deadly accuracy. Eldrin used his magic to create protective barriers, shielding the group from the worst of the attacks. Thorne's arrows flew true, each one finding its mark and weakening the creatures. Aeliana summoned vines from the ground, entangling the creatures and holding them in place.

Elara raised her staff, chanting a powerful incantation. A beam of light shot from her staff, striking the dark creatures and enveloping them in a shimmering aura. The creatures roared in pain, their bodies writhing as the light purified the darkness within them.

With a final, powerful push, the group managed to defeat the creatures and reach the exit. They burst out into the daylight, the fresh air filling their lungs and the warm sun on their faces.

"We made it," Elara said, her voice filled with relief. "We're safe."

Kael nodded, his expression softening. "But we need to keep moving. The fortress is collapsing, and we need to get as far away as possible."

They raced down the mountainside, the ground trembling beneath their feet as the fortress continued to collapse. The air was filled with the sound of cracking stone and the roar of falling debris. But they didn't stop, their determination driving them forward.

As they reached the base of the mountain, they turned to see the dark fortress crumble into a pile of rubble. The dark mage's reign of terror was over, and Eldoria was safe once more.

"We did it," Elara said, her voice filled with pride. "We saved Eldoria."

Kael placed a reassuring hand on her shoulder. "We did it together. And now, we can begin to rebuild."

The group stood together, their hearts swelling with a sense of accomplishment and hope. They had faced countless dangers and overcome seemingly insurmountable obstacles. Their bond had been tested, but it had not broken. They were stronger and more determined than ever.

As they looked out over the landscape, the sun setting in the distance, they knew that their journey was far from over. There would be new challenges and new adventures, but they were ready to face them together.

"We should rest," Kael said, his voice gentle but firm. "We'll need all our strength for the journey ahead."

They settled down for the night, each taking turns to keep watch. Elara lay beneath the stars, her mind racing with thoughts of the prophecy and the challenges that awaited them. She knew the path would be fraught with danger, but she was ready to face it.

In the quiet of the night, Elara felt a sense of peace. The prophecy had brought them together, and together, they had saved Eldoria. She closed her eyes, letting the sounds of the forest lull her to sleep, her heart filled with hope and determination.

The dawn broke with a soft, golden light, casting a warm glow over the landscape. Elara and her companions packed up their camp and prepared to continue their journey, their spirits high and their resolve unwavering.

As they set off towards their next destination, Elara felt a surge of excitement and anticipation. The journey ahead would be long and difficult, but they were ready to face whatever challenges lay in their path. Together, they would rebuild Eldoria and ensure that the darkness never returned. The final confrontation had tested their resolve, but they were stronger for it, and they were determined to see their mission through to the end.

Chapter 10: The Final Battle

The Gathering Storm

The group arrived at the battlefield, a vast plain stretching out under a darkening sky. Storm clouds gathered ominously, casting long shadows over the land. The air was thick with tension, the scent of rain mingling with the faint tang of magic. Elara, Kael, Lyra, Eldrin, Thorne, and Aeliana stood at the edge of the plain, their hearts pounding with a mix of fear and determination.

"This is it," Eldrin said, his voice barely audible over the distant rumble of thunder. "The final battle."

Elara nodded, her heart heavy with the weight of their mission. "We need to make our final preparations. The dark mage's forces will be upon us soon."

Kael drew his sword, the blade gleaming in the dim light. "Let's set up our defenses and strategize our approach. We need to be ready for anything."

The group moved quickly, setting up barriers and fortifications to protect their position. They worked in silence, the gravity of the situation hanging over them like a shroud. Each member of the group knew what was at stake, and they were determined to give everything they had to protect Eldoria.

As they worked, Elara couldn't help but notice the tension in the air. Doubts and fears began to surface, gnawing at the edges of their resolve. She could see it in the way Kael's hands trembled as he tightened his grip on his sword, in the way Lyra's eyes darted nervously around the battlefield, and in the way Eldrin's shoulders sagged under the weight of his responsibilities.

"We're facing an army," Thorne said, his voice filled with uncertainty. "How can we hope to win?"

Aeliana placed a reassuring hand on his shoulder, her eyes glowing softly. "We have faced many challenges and emerged stronger for it. Together, we are unstoppable."

Elara knew she needed to say something to rally their spirits. She took a deep breath, her heart pounding in her chest. "Listen to me," she said, her voice steady and filled with conviction. "We have come a long way. We have faced countless dangers and overcome seemingly insurmountable obstacles. We have fought for each other and for Eldoria. And now, we stand on the brink of victory."

She looked around at her friends, her eyes filled with determination. "The dark mage's forces may be powerful, but they do not have what we have. They do not have our bond, our courage, or our resolve. We fight not just for ourselves, but for everyone who cannot. We fight for the future of Eldoria."

Kael nodded, his expression hardening. "Elara's right. We have come too far to give up now. We will fight with everything we have, and we will win."

Lyra's eyes sparkled with determination. "For Eldoria."

Eldrin raised his staff, his voice filled with resolve. "For Eldoria."

Thorne and Aeliana echoed the sentiment, their voices strong and unwavering. "For Eldoria."

As the storm clouds gathered overhead, the group stood united, their spirits lifted by Elara's words. They knew the battle ahead would be fierce and chaotic, but they were ready to face it together. They had come too far to turn back now.

The distant rumble of thunder grew louder, and the first drops of rain began to fall, mingling with the sweat and dirt on their faces. The air was charged with electricity, the storm a reflection of the turmoil within their hearts.

Elara raised her staff, the light at its tip glowing brightly. "Let's do this. For Eldoria."

With their final preparations complete and their resolve strengthened, the group stood ready to face the dark mage's forces. The storm raged overhead, the wind howling and the rain pouring down in torrents. But they stood firm, their hearts filled with determination and their bond unbreakable.

The final battle was about to begin, and they were ready to give everything they had to protect Eldoria. Together, they would face the darkness and emerge victorious. The fate of their world rested in their hands, and they were determined to see their mission through to the end.

The First Clash

The storm raged overhead, lightning flashing across the darkened sky and thunder rumbling like the drums of war. The rain poured down in torrents, soaking the battlefield and turning the ground into a muddy quagmire. Elara, Kael, Lyra, Eldrin, Thorne, and Aeliana stood at the edge of the plain, their hearts pounding with anticipation and fear.

"This is it," Kael said, his voice barely audible over the roar of the storm. "The battle begins now."

Elara nodded, her heart heavy with the weight of their mission. "Stay together and watch each other's backs. We can do this."

As the dark mage's forces charged across the plain, a chaotic clash of steel and magic erupted. The air was filled with the sounds of battle—the clash of swords, the crackle of spells, and the cries of the wounded. The dark creatures moved with a predatory grace, their eyes glowing with a malevolent light.

Kael led the charge, his sword flashing in the dim light as he cut down the first wave of attackers. Lyra moved with her usual grace and agility, her daggers finding their mark with deadly accuracy. Eldrin used his magic to create protective barriers, shielding the group from the worst of the attacks. Thorne's arrows flew true, each one finding its mark and weakening the enemy's ranks. Aeliana summoned vines from the ground, entangling the dark creatures and holding them in place.

Elara raised her staff, chanting a powerful incantation. A beam of light shot from her staff, striking the dark creatures and enveloping them in a shimmering aura. The creatures roared in pain, their bodies writhing as the light purified the darkness within them.

But the battle was fierce and chaotic, and the group soon found themselves separated in the melee. Elara fought her way through the throng of enemies, her heart pounding with fear and determination. She could see Kael battling a group of dark creatures on the far side of the plain, his sword flashing in the dim light. Lyra was darting through the enemy ranks, her daggers flashing as she took down one foe after another. Eldrin was surrounded by a group of dark mages, his staff glowing brightly as he cast protective spells. Thorne and Aeliana were fighting side by side, their combined skills and magic holding the enemy at bay.

"We need to regroup!" Elara shouted, her voice barely audible over the roar of the storm. "Stay together!"

The group fought their way towards each other, their determination and resolve driving them forward. They used their skills and teamwork to overcome the initial onslaught, their bond stronger than ever. Despite the overwhelming odds, they managed to regroup and push back the dark mage's forces, gaining a foothold on the battlefield.

As they stood together, their hearts pounding with adrenaline, Elara felt a surge of hope. They had faced the first clash and emerged victorious, but she knew the battle was far from over.

"We need to keep moving," Kael said, his voice filled with determination. "The dark mage's stronghold is just ahead."

Elara nodded, her heart swelling with pride for her friends. "Let's do this. For Eldoria."

With their spirits lifted and their resolve strengthened, the group pressed forward, their hearts filled with determination and their bond unbreakable. The storm raged overhead, the wind howling and the rain pouring down in torrents. But they stood firm, their hearts filled with determination and their bond unbreakable.

The final battle had begun, and they were ready to give everything they had to protect Eldoria. Together, they would face the darkness and emerge victorious. The fate of their world rested in their hands, and they were determined to see their mission through to the end.

The Turning Point

The storm raged on, the sky dark and foreboding as lightning flashed and thunder roared. The battlefield was a chaotic sea of clashing steel and crackling magic, the air thick with the scent of rain and blood. Elara, Kael, Lyra, Eldrin, Thorne, and Aeliana fought with everything they had, their hearts pounding with determination and fear.

"We need to push forward!" Kael shouted, his voice barely audible over the din of battle. "The dark mage's stronghold is just ahead!"

Elara nodded, her staff glowing brightly as she cast a protective spell over her friends. "Stay together! We can do this!"

The group pressed on, their resolve unwavering as they fought their way through the dark mage's forces. The ground was slick with mud and blood, making each step a challenge. But they moved with purpose, their eyes fixed on the dark fortress that loomed in the distance.

As they neared the stronghold, they encountered the dark mage's elite guards—powerful enemies that moved with deadly precision. These were no ordinary soldiers; they were infused with dark magic, their eyes glowing with a sinister light.

"Get ready!" Kael shouted, raising his sword. "These are the dark mage's best warriors!"

The elite guards charged, their weapons gleaming in the dim light. The group met them head-on, their skills and teamwork tested to the limit. Kael's sword clashed with the guards' blades, each strike sending sparks flying. Lyra moved with her usual grace and agility, her daggers finding their mark with deadly accuracy. Eldrin used his magic to create protective barriers, shielding the group from the worst of the attacks. Thorne's arrows flew true, each one finding its mark and weakening the guards. Aeliana summoned vines from the ground, entangling the guards and holding them in place.

Elara raised her staff, chanting a powerful incantation. A beam of light shot from her staff, striking the elite guards and enveloping them in a shimmering aura. The guards roared in pain, their bodies writhing as the light purified the darkness within them.

"We need to work together!" Elara shouted, her voice filled with determination. "We can defeat them if we stay united!"

The group fought with everything they had, their resolve and unity unwavering. Each member played a crucial role in the fight, their combined strength and determination driving them forward. Despite the overwhelming odds, they managed to defeat the elite guards, their bodies dissolving into mist as the dark magic was purged from their souls.

"We did it," Kael said, his voice filled with relief. "But we need to keep moving. The dark mage is waiting for us."

Elara nodded, her heart pounding with anticipation. "Let's go. For Eldoria."

With the elite guards defeated and their spirits lifted, the group pressed on towards the dark mage's stronghold. The storm raged overhead, the wind howling and the rain pouring down in torrents. But they stood firm, their hearts filled with determination and their bond unbreakable.

As they reached the entrance to the stronghold, they could feel the dark mage's presence growing stronger. The air was thick with dark magic, and the ground trembled beneath their feet. The stronghold loomed before them, a dark and foreboding place filled with shadows and whispers.

"This is it," Eldrin said, his voice barely audible over the roar of the storm. "The final confrontation."

Elara took a deep breath, her heart heavy with the weight of their mission. "We need to be prepared. Malakar will be waiting for us."

Kael raised his sword, his eyes filled with resolve. "Let's do this. For Eldoria."

With their resolve strengthened and their bond unbreakable, the group entered the dark mage's stronghold, ready to face whatever challenges lay in their path. Together, they would confront the darkness and emerge victorious. The fate of their world rested in their hands, and they were determined to see their mission through to the end.

The Final Confrontation

The dark mage's stronghold was a place of shadows and whispers, its walls lined with dark tapestries and ancient artifacts that pulsed with malevolent energy. The air was thick with the scent of decay and the faint hum of dark magic. Elara, Kael, Lyra, Eldrin, Thorne, and Aeliana stood at the entrance, their hearts pounding with a mix of fear and determination.

"This is it," Eldrin said, his voice barely audible over the distant rumble of thunder. "The final confrontation."

Elara nodded, her heart heavy with the weight of their mission. "We need to be prepared. Malakar will be waiting for us."

Kael raised his sword, his eyes filled with resolve. "Let's do this. For Eldoria."

They stepped into the stronghold, the air growing colder and the light dimmer as they moved deeper inside. The walls were covered in intricate carvings and symbols, their surfaces slick with moisture. The ground was uneven and littered with debris, making each step a challenge.

As they ventured further, they could feel the dark mage's presence growing stronger. The air was thick with dark magic, and the ground trembled beneath their feet. The stronghold seemed to pulse with a malevolent energy, the shadows flickering and shifting as if alive.

Finally, they reached the dark mage's throne room, a grand and ominous chamber filled with dark energy. The air inside was thick with the scent of decay and the faint hum of dark magic. At the far end of the room, seated on a throne of black stone, was Malakar, the dark mage. His eyes glowed with a sinister light, and the air around him crackled with dark energy.

"Welcome, travelers," Malakar said, his voice cold and menacing. "I've been expecting you."

The group stood their ground, their weapons at the ready. "Your reign of terror ends here, Malakar," Elara said, her voice steady despite the fear gnawing at her insides.

Malakar laughed, a cold, hollow sound that echoed through the chamber. "You think you can defeat me? You are nothing but pawns in a game you cannot hope to win."

He raised his hand, and the air around them shimmered with dark energy. The ground trembled, and the walls seemed to close in around them. The group felt a wave of fear and doubt wash over them, their insecurities and fears brought to the surface.

"You are weak," Malakar said, his voice filled with contempt. "You cannot hope to defeat me."

Kael stepped forward, his sword raised. "We are stronger than you think. We will fight for Eldoria and for each other."

A fierce battle ensued, the air filled with the clash of metal and the crackle of magic. Malakar's dark energy was powerful and relentless, his attacks swift and deadly. But the group fought back with equal determination, their bond stronger than ever.

Kael's sword flashed in the dim light, each strike precise and powerful. Lyra moved with her usual grace and agility, her daggers finding their mark with deadly accuracy. Eldrin used his magic to create protective barriers, shielding the group from the worst of Malakar's attacks. Thorne's arrows flew true, each one finding its mark and weakening the dark mage's defenses. Aeliana summoned vines from the ground, entangling Malakar and holding him in place.

Elara raised her staff, chanting a powerful incantation. A beam of light shot from her staff, striking Malakar and enveloping him in a shimmering aura. Malakar roared in pain, his body writhing as the light purified the darkness within him.

"You cannot defeat me," Malakar snarled, his eyes filled with rage. "I will destroy you all."

Despite Malakar's efforts to break their spirit and turn them against each other, the group remained united. They fought with everything they had, their resolve and unity unwavering. They pushed Malakar back, their combined strength and determination driving him to the brink of defeat.

With a final, powerful strike, Kael drove his sword into Malakar's heart. The dark mage let out an agonized roar before collapsing to the ground, his body dissolving into mist.

"We did it," Elara said, her voice filled with relief. "But we need to be careful. Malakar may have been defeated, but his influence is still strong."

Kael nodded, his expression serious. "We need to ensure the safety of the relics and each other. The fortress is still dangerous."

With Malakar defeated and their bond stronger than ever, the group felt a renewed sense of purpose. They had faced the dark mage and emerged victorious, but they knew the journey ahead would be long and difficult. Together, they would protect the relics and save Eldoria from the encroaching darkness. The final confrontation had tested their resolve, but they were determined to see their mission through to the end.

Victory and Sacrifice

The dark mage's throne room was eerily silent, the air still thick with the remnants of dark magic. Malakar's body had dissolved into mist, leaving behind only the faint echo of his malevolent presence. Elara, Kael, Lyra, Eldrin, Thorne, and Aeliana stood in the center of the chamber, their hearts pounding with a mix of relief and exhaustion.

"We did it," Elara said, her voice trembling with emotion. "Malakar is defeated."

Kael nodded, his expression serious. "But we can't let our guard down. The fortress is still dangerous, and we need to get out of here."

As if on cue, the ground beneath their feet began to tremble, and the walls of the fortress shuddered. The dark magic that had held the structure together was unraveling, and the fortress was beginning to collapse.

"We need to move, now!" Kael shouted, his voice cutting through the growing chaos.

The group sprang into action, their movements swift and coordinated. They raced through the crumbling corridors, the ground shaking beneath their feet and debris falling around them. The air was filled with the sound of cracking stone and the roar of collapsing walls.

Elara led the way, her staff glowing brightly to light their path. She could feel the fortress's defenses activating in a final attempt to trap them, but she was determined to get her friends to safety.

As they reached the entrance to the tunnel, a massive stone block fell from the ceiling, blocking their path. "We need to find another way out!" Lyra shouted, her eyes scanning the collapsing structure.

Eldrin raised his hands, chanting a series of incantations. The stone block shimmered and began to dissolve, creating a narrow passageway. "This way!" he called, his voice filled with urgency.

They squeezed through the passageway, the ground trembling beneath their feet. The tunnel was filled with dust and debris, making it difficult to see and breathe. But they pressed on, their determination driving them forward.

As they neared the end of the tunnel, they could see the faint glow of daylight. "We're almost there!" Thorne shouted, his voice filled with hope.

But just as they were about to reach the exit, a series of dark creatures emerged from the shadows, their eyes glowing with a malevolent light. "We need to fight our way through!" Kael shouted, his sword flashing in the dim light.

A fierce battle ensued, the air filled with the clash of metal and the crackle of magic. The dark creatures were relentless, their attacks swift and deadly. But the group fought back with equal determination, their bond stronger than ever.

Kael's sword flashed in the dim light, each strike precise and powerful. Lyra moved with her usual grace and agility, her daggers finding their mark with deadly accuracy. Eldrin used his magic to create protective barriers, shielding the group from the worst of the attacks. Thorne's arrows flew true, each one finding its mark and weakening the creatures. Aeliana summoned vines from the ground, entangling the creatures and holding them in place.

Elara raised her staff, chanting a powerful incantation. A beam of light shot from her staff, striking the dark creatures and enveloping them in a shimmering aura. The creatures roared in pain, their bodies writhing as the light purified the darkness within them.

With a final, powerful push, the group managed to defeat the creatures and reach the exit. They burst out into the daylight, the fresh air filling their lungs and the warm sun on their faces.

"We made it," Elara said, her voice filled with relief. "We're safe."

Kael nodded, his expression softening. "But we need to keep moving. The fortress is collapsing, and we need to get as far away as possible."

They raced down the mountainside, the ground trembling beneath their feet as the fortress continued to collapse. The air was filled with the sound of cracking stone and the roar of falling debris. But they didn't stop, their determination driving them forward.

As they reached the base of the mountain, they turned to see the dark fortress crumble into a pile of rubble. The dark mage's reign of terror was over, and Eldoria was safe once more.

"We did it," Elara said, her voice filled with pride. "We saved Eldoria."

Kael placed a reassuring hand on her shoulder. "We did it together. And now, we can begin to rebuild."

The group stood together, their hearts swelling with a sense of accomplishment and hope. They had faced countless dangers and overcome seemingly insurmountable obstacles. Their bond had been tested, but it had not broken. They were stronger and more determined than ever.

As they looked out over the landscape, the sun setting in the distance, they knew that their journey was far from over. There would be new challenges and new adventures, but they were ready to face them together.

"We should rest," Kael said, his voice gentle but firm. "We'll need all our strength for the journey ahead."

They settled down for the night, each taking turns to keep watch. Elara lay beneath the stars, her mind racing with thoughts of the prophecy and the challenges that awaited them. She knew the path would be fraught with danger, but she was ready to face it.

In the quiet of the night, Elara felt a sense of peace. The prophecy had brought them together, and together, they had saved Eldoria. She closed her eyes, letting the sounds of the forest lull her to sleep, her heart filled with hope and determination.

The dawn broke with a soft, golden light, casting a warm glow over the landscape. Elara and her companions packed up their camp and prepared to continue their journey, their spirits high and their resolve unwavering.

As they set off towards their next destination, Elara felt a surge of excitement and anticipation. The journey ahead would be long and difficult, but they were ready to face whatever challenges lay in their path. Together, they would rebuild Eldoria and ensure that the darkness never returned. The final confrontation had tested their resolve, but they were stronger for it, and they were determined to see their mission through to the end.

12

Chapter 11: The Aftermath

The Return to Eldenwood

The journey back to Eldenwood was filled with a mix of relief and sorrow. The group moved through the familiar landscape, their hearts heavy with the memories of the battles they had fought and the friends they had lost. The air was crisp and cool, the scent of pine and earth filling their lungs as they approached their home village.

As they crested the final hill, Eldenwood came into view. The village, once vibrant and full of life, now lay in ruins. The dark mage's influence had left its mark, with homes reduced to rubble and the land scarred by dark magic. The sight was a stark reminder of the cost of their victory.

"We're home," Elara said, her voice filled with a mix of relief and sadness. "But there's so much work to be done."

Kael nodded, his expression grim. "We need to start rebuilding. The villagers will need our help."

As they entered the village, they were greeted by the re-maining villagers, their faces etched with a mixture of re-lief and wariness. The villagers had endured much during the dark mage's reign, and while they were grateful for the group's return, they were also uncertain about what the future held.

"Elara, Kael, you're back!" Maren, the village healer, ex-claimed, her eyes filling with tears. "We were so worried. Is it over? Is the dark mage truly defeated?"

Elara nodded, her heart swelling with determination. "Yes, Malakar is defeated. But we have a lot of work to do to rebuild our home."

The villagers gathered around, their expressions a mix of hope and uncertainty. Elara could see the fear and doubt in their eyes, and she knew they needed reassurance.

"We've faced many challenges and overcome them to-gether," Elara said, her voice steady and filled with con-viction. "We will rebuild Eldenwood, and we will make it stronger than ever. But we need to work together, as a com-munity."

Kael stepped forward, his presence commanding and re-assuring. "We will help you rebuild. We will repair the homes, restore the land, and ensure that Eldenwood thrives once more."

Lyra, Eldrin, Thorne, and Aeliana joined them, their ex-pressions filled with determination. "We're in this together," Lyra said, her voice strong. "We'll do whatever it takes to re-store our home."

The villagers nodded, their spirits lifting as they saw the resolve in the group's eyes. They began to organize themselves, each person taking on tasks to help with the rebuilding efforts. The air was filled with the sounds of hammers and saws, the scent of fresh wood mingling with the earthy aroma of the land.

Elara and her friends worked tirelessly alongside the villagers, their hearts swelling with a sense of purpose. They repaired homes, cleared debris, and planted new crops. The physical labor was exhausting, but it was also healing, a way to channel their grief and sorrow into something positive.

As the days passed, the village began to take shape once more. The scars left by the dark mage's influence were slowly being healed, and a sense of hope and renewal filled the air. The villagers worked together, their bond strengthened by the trials they had faced.

One evening, as the sun set over the village, casting a warm golden light over the landscape, Elara stood at the edge of the village, looking out over the progress they had made. Kael joined her, his expression thoughtful.

"We've come a long way," Kael said, his voice filled with pride. "But there's still much to be done."

Elara nodded, her heart swelling with determination. "We'll get there. Together, we can rebuild Eldenwood and ensure that the darkness never returns."

Kael placed a reassuring hand on her shoulder. "We will. And we'll do it together."

As the stars began to twinkle in the night sky, Elara felt a sense of peace settle over her. They had faced countless challenges and overcome seemingly insurmountable obstacles. Their bond had been tested, but it had not broken. They were stronger and more determined than ever.

With renewed hope and determination, Elara and her friends continued their work, their hearts filled with the promise of a brighter future. Together, they would rebuild Eldenwood and ensure that the darkness never returned. The journey ahead would be long and difficult, but they were ready to face it together, their bond unbreakable and their resolve unwavering.

Honoring the Fallen

The sun rose slowly over Eldenwood, casting a soft, golden light over the village. The air was filled with the scent of fresh earth and blooming flowers, a stark contrast to the devastation that had once plagued their home. The villagers had worked tirelessly to rebuild, and now it was time to honor those who had given their lives in the battle against the dark mage.

A solemn ceremony was held in the village square, the heart of Eldenwood. The villagers gathered, their faces etched with grief and determination. A large stone monument had been erected in the center of the square, inscribed with the names of the fallen. Flowers and candles surrounded the monument, their soft glow a tribute to the lives lost.

Elara stood at the front of the gathering, her heart heavy with sorrow. She looked out at the faces of her friends and neighbors, each one bearing the weight of their losses. Kael, Lyra, Eldrin, Thorne, and Aeliana stood beside her, their expressions somber.

"We are here today to honor those who gave their lives to protect Eldoria," Elara began, her voice steady despite the lump in her throat. "They fought bravely and selflessly, and their sacrifice will never be forgotten."

Kael stepped forward, his eyes filled with grief and determination. "We owe them a debt that can never be repaid. But we can honor their memory by continuing to fight for the future they believed in."

Lyra's voice trembled as she spoke. "They were our friends, our family. They gave everything to protect us. We must ensure that their sacrifice was not in vain."

Eldrin raised his staff, the light at its tip glowing softly. "We will remember them always. Their courage and strength will guide us as we rebuild Eldoria."

Thorne and Aeliana added their voices to the tribute, each word a testament to the bond they shared with the fallen. The villagers listened in silence, their hearts heavy with grief but also filled with a sense of unity and purpose.

As the ceremony continued, the group grappled with their emotions, each member dealing with their grief in their own way. Elara felt a deep ache in her chest, the weight of their losses pressing down on her. She knew she needed to be strong for her friends and for the village, but the pain was almost too much to bear.

Kael placed a reassuring hand on her shoulder, his eyes filled with understanding. "It's okay to grieve, Elara. We all need to mourn our losses."

Elara nodded, her eyes filling with tears. "I just... I wish we could have saved them all."

Lyra stepped forward, her voice gentle. "We did everything we could. And now, we must honor their memory by continuing to fight for the future they believed in."

Eldrin's voice was filled with wisdom. "Grief is a part of healing. We must allow ourselves to feel it, but we must also find the strength to move forward."

Thorne and Aeliana nodded in agreement, their expressions filled with determination. "We will rebuild Eldoria," Thorne said, his voice strong. "For them."

As the ceremony drew to a close, the villagers placed flowers and candles at the base of the monument, each one a symbol of their love and respect for the fallen. The air was filled with the soft glow of candlelight and the scent of blooming flowers, a tribute to the lives lost and the hope for a brighter future.

Elara stood before the monument, her heart swelling with a mix of grief and determination. She knew the journey ahead would be long and difficult, but she was ready to face it with her friends by her side. Together, they would honor the fallen and rebuild Eldoria, ensuring that the darkness never returned.

As the sun set over Eldenwood, casting a warm golden light over the village, Elara felt a sense of peace settle over her. They had faced countless challenges and overcome seemingly insurmountable obstacles. Their bond had been tested, but it had not broken. They were stronger and more determined than ever.

With renewed hope and determination, Elara and her friends continued their work, their hearts filled with the promise of a brighter future. Together, they would rebuild

Eldoria and ensure that the darkness never returned. The journey ahead would be long and difficult, but they were ready to face it together, their bond unbreakable and their resolve unwavering.

Rebuilding and Healing

The days following the ceremony were filled with hard work and determination. The villagers of Eldenwood, alongside Elara, Kael, Lyra, Eldrin, Thorne, and Aeliana, threw themselves into the task of rebuilding their home. The air was filled with the sounds of hammers and saws, the scent of fresh wood mingling with the earthy aroma of the land.

Elara worked tirelessly, her hands calloused and her muscles aching from the physical labor. She helped repair homes, clear debris, and plant new crops. The work was exhausting, but it was also healing, a way to channel her grief and sorrow into something positive.

Kael was a constant presence by her side, his strength and determination a source of inspiration for the villagers. He led the efforts to rebuild the village's defenses, ensuring that Eldenwood would be protected from any future threats. His leadership and unwavering resolve gave the villagers hope and a sense of security.

Lyra used her agility and quick reflexes to navigate the more precarious tasks, such as repairing rooftops and clearing fallen trees. Her sharp wit and infectious laughter lightened the mood, bringing a sense of camaraderie and joy to the hard work.

Eldrin's knowledge of ancient magic proved invaluable in restoring the land. He used his spells to heal the soil, purify the water, and encourage the growth of new plants. His wisdom and gentle guidance helped the villagers reconnect with the magic of Eldoria, fostering a sense of renewal and hope.

Thorne and Aeliana worked together to restore the village's gardens and orchards. Thorne's skills as a ranger and Aeliana's connection to nature made them a formidable team. They planted new seeds, tended to the plants, and ensured that the village would have a bountiful harvest in the coming seasons.

Despite their progress, the physical and emotional toll of the battle weighed heavily on them. Each member of the group grappled with their own grief and exhaustion, finding solace and strength in their shared purpose. They supported each other through the difficult moments, their bond growing stronger with each passing day.

One afternoon, as the sun cast a warm golden light over the village, Elara took a moment to rest and reflect. She sat on a fallen log, her eyes scanning the bustling activity around her. The villagers were working together, their faces filled with determination and hope. It was a sight that filled her heart with pride.

Kael joined her, his expression thoughtful. "We've come a long way," he said, his voice filled with pride. "But there's still much to be done."

Elara nodded, her heart swelling with determination. "We'll get there. Together, we can rebuild Eldenwood and ensure that the darkness never returns."

Lyra approached, her eyes sparkling with mischief. "Taking a break, are we? I thought you were the one who said we needed to keep working."

Elara laughed, the sound light and joyful. "Just a moment of rest. We all need it."

Eldrin joined them, his staff glowing softly. "Rest is important. We must take care of ourselves if we are to take care of others."

Thorne and Aeliana arrived, their hands covered in dirt and their faces flushed with exertion. "The gardens are coming along nicely," Thorne said, his voice filled with satisfaction. "We'll have a good harvest this year."

Aeliana nodded, her eyes glowing with a soft, inner light. "The land is healing, just as we are. Together, we will restore Eldoria."

As they sat together, sharing stories and laughter, Elara felt a sense of peace settle over her. They had faced countless challenges and overcome seemingly insurmountable obstacles. Their bond had been tested, but it had not broken. They were stronger and more determined than ever.

With renewed hope and determination, Elara and her friends continued their work, their hearts filled with the promise of a brighter future. Together, they would rebuild Eldenwood and ensure that the darkness never returned. The journey ahead would be long and difficult, but they were ready to face it together, their bond unbreakable and their resolve unwavering.

The Council's Decision

The sun was high in the sky as Elara, Kael, Lyra, Eldrin, Thorne, and Aeliana made their way to the ancient sanctuary where the remnants of the magical council awaited them. The air was filled with the scent of blooming flowers and the soft hum of magic, a stark contrast to the devastation they had faced in recent weeks. The journey to the sanctuary was filled with a mix of anticipation and uncertainty, each member of the group grappling with their own thoughts and fears about the future.

As they approached the sanctuary, the towering stone pillars covered in intricate runes came into view. The sanctuary was a place of ancient power and wisdom, its walls lined with shelves of ancient tomes and artifacts. The air inside was cool and refreshing, a welcome respite from the heat of the day.

The council members were already gathered around a large, circular table in the center of the room. Thalindra, the wise and aged elf, Borin, the stout and sturdy dwarf, and Seraphina, the ethereal and enigmatic fae, looked up as the group entered, their expressions a mix of relief and concern.

"Welcome, Elara and friends," Thalindra said, her voice soft but commanding. "We are glad you have come. The time has come to discuss the future of Eldoria and the role you will play in its restoration."

Elara nodded, her heart pounding with anticipation. "We are ready to do whatever it takes to rebuild Eldoria and ensure that the darkness never returns."

Borin's expression was serious as he spoke. "The battle against Malakar was only the beginning. There is much work to be done to restore the balance of magic and rebuild our world."

Seraphina's eyes glowed with a soft, inner light as she added, "Each of you has shown great courage and strength. But the path ahead will be fraught with challenges. We must come to a consensus about your roles and how best to serve Eldoria in the aftermath of the battle."

The group exchanged glances, each member grappling with their own doubts and fears. Elara could see the uncertainty in their eyes, and she knew they needed to have an open and honest discussion about their responsibilities and the path forward.

Kael was the first to speak, his voice steady but filled with emotion. "I believe our first priority should be to ensure the safety and security of Eldoria. We need to rebuild our defenses and protect our people from any future threats."

Lyra nodded in agreement. "And we need to continue to support the villagers as they rebuild their homes and their lives. They have been through so much, and they need our help to heal and move forward."

Eldrin's expression was thoughtful as he added, "We must also focus on restoring the balance of magic. The dark mage's influence has left its mark on the land, and we need to heal the soil, purify the water, and encourage the growth of new plants."

Thorne's voice was filled with determination as he said, "And we need to ensure that the knowledge and wisdom of the past are preserved. We must protect the ancient tomes and artifacts that hold the secrets of our world."

Aeliana's presence was a calming force as she spoke. "We must also foster a sense of unity and hope among the people. They need to know that we are here for them, and that we will work together to rebuild Eldoria."

Thalindra nodded, her eyes filled with approval. "You have all spoken wisely. The path ahead will be difficult, but I have no doubt that you will rise to the challenge."

Borin's expression softened as he added, "You have proven yourselves to be true leaders. Your courage and determination will guide us as we rebuild our world."

Seraphina's voice was filled with warmth as she said, "We will support you in any way we can. Together, we will restore Eldoria and ensure that the darkness never returns."

The group felt a sense of relief and determination as they listened to the council's words. They knew the journey ahead would be long and difficult, but they were ready to face it together. Their bond had been tested, but it had not broken. They were stronger and more determined than ever.

As they left the sanctuary, the sun was beginning to set, casting a warm golden light over the landscape. Elara felt a sense of peace settle over her. They had faced countless challenges and overcome seemingly insurmountable obstacles. Their bond had been tested, but it had not broken. They were stronger and more determined than ever.

With renewed hope and determination, Elara and her friends continued their work, their hearts filled with the promise of a brighter future. Together, they would rebuild

Eldoria and ensure that the darkness never returned. The journey ahead would be long and difficult, but they were ready to face it together, their bond unbreakable and their resolve unwavering.

A New Beginning

The sun rose over Eldenwood, casting a warm, golden light over the village. The air was filled with the scent of blooming flowers and the soft hum of magic, a testament to the hard work and determination of the villagers and their protectors. Elara, Kael, Lyra, Eldrin, Thorne, and Aeliana stood at the edge of the village, looking out over the restored homes and the land beyond.

"We've come a long way," Elara said, her voice filled with pride and a touch of sadness. "But there's still so much to do."

Kael nodded, his expression thoughtful. "We've faced countless challenges and made many sacrifices. But we've also forged bonds that will never be broken."

Lyra's eyes sparkled with determination. "And we've shown that no matter how dark things get, we can always find the light."

Eldrin raised his staff, the light at its tip glowing softly. "The balance of magic is being restored, and Eldoria is healing. But we must remain vigilant and continue to protect our world."

Thorne's voice was filled with resolve. "We will honor the memory of those we've lost by ensuring that their sacrifices were not in vain."

Aeliana's presence was a calming force, her eyes glowing with a soft, inner light. "Together, we will rebuild Eldoria and ensure that the darkness never returns."

As they stood together, reflecting on their journey and the challenges they had faced, Elara felt a sense of peace settle over her. They had come a long way since leaving Eldenwood, and the journey ahead would be filled with uncertainty. But she knew they were ready to face whatever challenges lay in their path.

"We've learned so much and grown stronger because of it," Elara said, her voice filled with determination. "We will continue to fight for Eldoria and protect our home."

Kael placed a reassuring hand on her shoulder. "And we'll do it together. No matter what comes our way, we'll face it as a team."

Lyra smiled, her eyes filled with hope. "We've proven that we can overcome anything as long as we stand together."

Eldrin's voice was filled with wisdom. "The future is uncertain, but we have the strength and the knowledge to shape it for the better."

Thorne's expression was resolute. "We'll ensure that Eldoria remains a place of light and hope for generations to come."

Aeliana's voice was like a gentle breeze. "And we will always remember the lessons we've learned and the bonds we've forged."

As the sun continued to rise, casting a warm glow over the landscape, the group felt a renewed sense of purpose. They had faced countless dangers and overcome seemingly insurmountable obstacles. Their bond had been tested, but it had not broken. They were stronger and more determined than ever.

With renewed hope and determination, Elara and her friends set out on a new journey, ready to face whatever challenges lay ahead. Together, they would rebuild Eldoria and ensure that the darkness never returned. The journey ahead would be long and difficult, but they were ready to face it together, their bond unbreakable and their resolve unwavering.

As they walked away from Eldenwood, the village behind them a symbol of hope and renewal, Elara felt a sense of excitement and anticipation. The future was uncertain, but she knew they were ready to face it together. They had saved Eldoria from the darkness, and now they would work to ensure that it remained a place of light and hope for generations to come.

The final confrontation had tested their resolve, but they were stronger for it. And as they set off towards their next destination, their hearts were filled with the promise of a brighter future. Together, they would face whatever challenges lay ahead, their bond unbreakable and their resolve unwavering. The journey was far from over, but they were ready to face it together, their hearts filled with hope and determination.

13

Epilogue: A New Dawn

A Time of Peace

Eldenwood had transformed. The village, once ravaged by the dark mage's influence, now thrived with life and energy. The homes were rebuilt, the fields were lush with crops, and the air was filled with the sounds of laughter and the hum of daily activity. The villagers moved about with a sense of purpose and joy, their faces reflecting the peace that had finally settled over their home.

Elara stood at the edge of the village square, watching the bustling scene before her. Children played in the streets, their laughter ringing out like music. Farmers tended to their fields, their hands working the soil with care. The market was alive with the chatter of merchants and customers, the scent of fresh bread and blooming flowers mingling in the air.

"We did it," Elara said softly, her heart swelling with pride. "We brought Eldenwood back to life."

Kael stood beside her, his expression thoughtful. "It wasn't easy, but we did it together. And now, we can finally enjoy the peace we've fought so hard for."

Lyra approached, her eyes sparkling with joy. "It's amazing to see everyone so happy. We've come a long way."

Eldrin joined them, his staff glowing softly. "The balance of magic is being restored, and Eldoria is healing. But we must remain vigilant and continue to protect our world."

Thorne and Aeliana arrived, their faces filled with contentment. "The gardens are flourishing," Thorne said, his voice filled with satisfaction. "We'll have a bountiful harvest this year."

Aeliana nodded, her eyes glowing with a soft, inner light. "The land is healing, just as we are. Together, we will ensure that Eldoria remains a place of light and hope."

As they stood together, reflecting on the journey they had taken and the battles they had fought, Elara felt a sense of peace settle over her. They had faced countless challenges and overcome seemingly insurmountable obstacles. Their bond had been tested, but it had not broken. They were stronger and more determined than ever.

"We've all changed," Elara said, her voice filled with reflection. "We've grown stronger, wiser. But we've also had to make sacrifices."

Kael's expression was somber as he nodded. "We've lost friends and faced our own fears. But we've also found a sense of purpose and fulfillment."

Lyra's eyes were filled with determination. "And we've shown that no matter how dark things get, we can always find the light."

Eldrin's voice was filled with wisdom. "The journey has been difficult, but it has also brought us closer together. We are a family now, bound by our shared experiences and our love for Eldoria."

Thorne's voice was resolute. "We will honor the memory of those we've lost by ensuring that their sacrifices were not in vain."

Aeliana's presence was a calming force, her eyes glowing with a soft, inner light. "Together, we will rebuild Eldoria and ensure that the darkness never returns."

As they stood together, reflecting on their journey and the changes in their lives, Elara felt a sense of peace and fulfillment. They had made a difference, not just for themselves, but for the entire village. They had brought hope and light back to Eldenwood, and they were ready to face whatever challenges lay ahead.

"We've learned so much and grown stronger because of it," Elara said, her voice filled with determination. "We will continue to fight for Eldoria and protect our home."

Kael placed a reassuring hand on her shoulder. "And we'll do it together. No matter what comes our way, we'll face it as a team."

Lyra smiled, her eyes filled with hope. "We've proven that we can overcome anything as long as we stand together."

Eldrin's voice was filled with wisdom. "The future is uncertain, but we have the strength and the knowledge to shape it for the better."

Thorne's expression was resolute. "We'll ensure that Eldoria remains a place of light and hope for generations to come."

Aeliana's voice was like a gentle breeze. "And we will always remember the lessons we've learned and the bonds we've forged."

As the sun continued to rise, casting a warm glow over the landscape, the group felt a renewed sense of purpose. They had faced countless dangers and overcome seemingly insurmountable obstacles. Their bond had been tested, but it had not broken. They were stronger and more determined than ever.

With renewed hope and determination, Elara and her friends set out on a new journey, ready to face whatever challenges lay ahead. Together, they would rebuild Eldoria and ensure that the darkness never returned. The journey ahead would be long and difficult, but they were ready to face it together, their bond unbreakable and their resolve unwavering.

As they walked away from Eldenwood, the village behind them a symbol of hope and renewal, Elara felt a sense of excitement and anticipation. The future was uncertain, but she knew they were ready to face it together. They had saved Eldoria from the darkness, and now they would work to ensure that it remained a place of light and hope for generations to come. The final confrontation had tested their resolve, but they were stronger for it, and they were determined to see their mission through to the end.

The Legacy of the Fallen

The sun was setting over Eldenwood, casting a warm, golden light over the village. The air was filled with the scent of blooming flowers and the soft hum of magic. In the heart of the village, a memorial garden had been created, a place of peace and reflection dedicated to those who had lost their lives in the battle against the dark mage.

Elara stood at the entrance to the garden, her heart heavy with sorrow. The garden was filled with vibrant flowers and lush greenery, a stark contrast to the devastation they had faced. A large stone monument stood in the center, inscribed with the names of the fallen. Candles and flowers surrounded the monument, their soft glow a tribute to the lives lost.

Kael, Lyra, Eldrin, Thorne, and Aeliana joined her, their expressions somber. They had all lost friends and comrades in the battle, and the weight of their sacrifices hung heavily over them.

"We've come to honor their memory," Elara said, her voice trembling with emotion. "They gave everything to protect Eldoria. We must ensure that their sacrifices are never forgotten."

Kael nodded, his eyes filled with grief. "They were our friends, our family. We owe them a debt that can never be repaid."

Lyra's voice was filled with determination. "We will honor their legacy by continuing to fight for the future they believed in."

Eldrin raised his staff, the light at its tip glowing softly. "Their courage and strength will guide us as we rebuild Eldoria."

Thorne's voice was resolute. "We will remember them always. Their sacrifices will not be in vain."

Aeliana's presence was a calming force, her eyes glowing with a soft, inner light. "Together, we will ensure that their memory lives on."

As they stood together, reflecting on the lives lost and the sacrifices made, Elara felt a deep ache in her chest. The pain of their losses was almost too much to bear, but she knew they needed to find a way to honor their friends while also moving forward.

"We need to create a space of remembrance and reflection," Elara said, her voice filled with resolve. "A place where we can come to honor their memory and find solace in our grief."

Kael's expression softened as he nodded. "A memorial garden. A place of peace and reflection."

Lyra's eyes sparkled with determination. "We can plant flowers and trees, create a space where their memory can thrive."

Eldrin's voice was filled with wisdom. "We can inscribe their names on the monument, a lasting tribute to their bravery and sacrifice."

Thorne's voice was resolute. "And we can hold ceremonies and gatherings, a way to come together and remember."

Aeliana's presence was a calming force, her eyes glowing with a soft, inner light. "Together, we will create a space of healing and remembrance."

As they worked together to create the memorial garden, the villagers joined them, their hearts filled with a sense of purpose and unity. They planted flowers and trees, inscribed the names of the fallen on the monument, and created a space of peace and reflection.

The garden became a place of solace and healing, a place where the villagers could come to honor the memory of their friends and find comfort in their grief. The air was filled with the scent of blooming flowers and the soft hum of magic, a testament to the love and respect they held for the fallen.

One evening, as the sun set over the garden, casting a warm golden light over the landscape, Elara stood before the monument, her heart swelling with a mix of grief and determination. She knew the journey ahead would be long and difficult, but she was ready to face it with her friends by her side.

"We will honor their memory by continuing to fight for the future they believed in," Elara said, her voice filled with resolve. "Together, we will rebuild Eldoria and ensure that the darkness never returns."

Kael placed a reassuring hand on her shoulder. "We will. And we'll do it together."

Lyra smiled, her eyes filled with hope. "We've proven that we can overcome anything as long as we stand together."

Eldrin's voice was filled with wisdom. "The future is uncertain, but we have the strength and the knowledge to shape it for the better."

Thorne's expression was resolute. "We'll ensure that Eldoria remains a place of light and hope for generations to come."

Aeliana's voice was like a gentle breeze. "And we will always remember the lessons we've learned and the bonds we've forged."

As the stars began to twinkle in the night sky, Elara felt a sense of peace settle over her. They had faced countless challenges and overcome seemingly insurmountable obstacles. Their bond had been tested, but it had not broken. They were stronger and more determined than ever.

With renewed hope and determination, Elara and her friends continued their work, their hearts filled with the promise of a brighter future. Together, they would rebuild Eldoria and ensure that the darkness never returned. The journey ahead would be long and difficult, but they were ready to face it together, their bond unbreakable and their resolve unwavering.

The Next Generation

The sun shone brightly over Eldenwood, casting a warm, golden light over the village. The air was filled with the sounds of laughter and the hum of activity as the villagers went about their daily lives. In a clearing on the outskirts of the village, a group of young villagers gathered, their faces filled with excitement and determination. They were the next generation of protectors, eager to learn the skills and knowledge needed to defend their home.

Elara stood at the edge of the clearing, watching the young villagers with a sense of pride and hope. She had taken on the role of mentor, guiding the next generation and passing on the lessons she had learned during her journey. Kael, Lyra, Eldrin, Thorne, and Aeliana stood beside her, each of them ready to share their expertise and support the young villagers.

"Are you ready?" Elara asked, her voice filled with encouragement.

The young villagers nodded eagerly, their eyes shining with determination. They were ready to learn, to train, and to become the protectors Eldoria needed.

Kael stepped forward, his presence commanding and reassuring. "Today, we will begin with combat training. It's important to be strong and agile, but also to work as a team. Remember, we are stronger together."

He demonstrated a series of combat moves, his sword flashing in the sunlight. The young villagers watched in awe, their eyes wide with admiration. Kael's movements were precise and powerful, a testament to his years of training and experience.

Lyra took over, her agility and quick reflexes a source of inspiration for the young villagers. She showed them how to move swiftly and silently, how to use their surroundings to their advantage. Her sharp wit and infectious laughter lightened the mood, bringing a sense of camaraderie and joy to the training.

Eldrin's knowledge of magic was invaluable. He taught the young villagers how to harness their magical abilities, how to cast protective spells and heal the land. His wisdom and gentle guidance helped them connect with the magic of Eldoria, fostering a sense of renewal and hope.

Thorne and Aeliana worked together to teach the young villagers about nature and survival. Thorne's skills as a ranger and Aeliana's connection to the natural world made them a formidable team. They showed the young villagers how to track animals, find food and water, and navigate the wilderness.

As the training continued, Elara watched with a sense of pride and fulfillment. The young villagers were eager to learn, their faces filled with determination and hope. They were the future of Eldoria, and she knew they would rise to the challenge.

One afternoon, as the sun began to set, casting a warm golden light over the clearing, Elara gathered the young villagers around her. "You've all done an incredible job today," she said, her voice filled with pride. "You've shown courage, determination, and a willingness to learn. These are the qualities that will make you great protectors of Eldoria."

Kael nodded in agreement. "Remember, we are stronger together. Always support each other and work as a team."

Lyra's eyes sparkled with encouragement. "And never forget to find joy in what you do. Laughter and camaraderie are just as important as strength and skill."

Eldrin's voice was filled with wisdom. "The magic of Eldoria is a gift. Use it wisely and with respect, and it will guide you."

Thorne's expression was resolute. "Nature is our ally. Learn from it, respect it, and it will provide for you."

Aeliana's presence was a calming force, her eyes glowing with a soft, inner light. "Together, we will ensure that Eldoria remains a place of light and hope."

As the young villagers listened to their mentors, their hearts swelled with pride and determination. They knew they had a responsibility to protect their home, and they were ready to rise to the challenge.

Elara felt a sense of peace settle over her. They had faced countless challenges and overcome seemingly insurmountable obstacles. Their bond had been tested, but it had not broken. They were stronger and more determined than ever.

With renewed hope and determination, Elara and her friends continued their work, their hearts filled with the promise of a brighter future. Together, they would guide the next generation and ensure that the darkness never returned. The journey ahead would be long and difficult, but they were ready to face it together, their bond unbreakable and their resolve unwavering.

As the stars began to twinkle in the night sky, Elara looked out over the clearing, her heart swelling with pride. The future of Eldoria was in good hands, and she knew they were ready to face whatever challenges lay ahead. Together, they would protect their home and ensure that it remained a place of light and hope for generations to come.

The final confrontation had tested their resolve, but they were stronger for it, and they were determined to see their mission through to the end.

A New Council

The ancient sanctuary stood as a testament to the enduring strength and wisdom of Eldoria. Its towering stone pillars, covered in intricate runes, glowed softly in the afternoon light. The air was filled with the scent of blooming flowers and the faint hum of magic, creating an atmosphere of peace and reverence. Elara, Kael, Lyra, Eldrin, Thorne, and Aeliana approached the sanctuary with a mix of anticipation and uncertainty.

Inside, the remnants of the magical council awaited them. Thalindra, the wise and aged elf, Borin, the stout and sturdy dwarf, and Seraphina, the ethereal and enigmatic fae, stood around a large, circular table in the center of the room. Their expressions were a blend of relief and concern as they welcomed the group.

"Welcome, Elara and friends," Thalindra said, her voice soft but commanding. "We are glad you have come. The time has come to discuss the future of Eldoria and the role you will play in its restoration."

Elara nodded, her heart pounding with anticipation. "We are ready to do whatever it takes to rebuild Eldoria and ensure that the darkness never returns."

Borin's expression was serious as he spoke. "The battle against Malakar was only the beginning. There is much work to be done to restore the balance of magic and rebuild our world."

Seraphina's eyes glowed with a soft, inner light as she added, "Each of you has shown great courage and strength. But the path ahead will be fraught with challenges. We must come to a consensus about your roles and how best to serve Eldoria in the aftermath of the battle."

The group exchanged glances, each member grappling with their own doubts and fears. Elara could see the uncertainty in their eyes, and she knew they needed to have an open and honest discussion about their responsibilities and the path forward.

Kael was the first to speak, his voice steady but filled with emotion. "I believe our first priority should be to ensure the safety and security of Eldoria. We need to rebuild our defenses and protect our people from any future threats."

Lyra nodded in agreement. "And we need to continue to support the villagers as they rebuild their homes and their lives. They have been through so much, and they need our help to heal and move forward."

Eldrin's expression was thoughtful as he added, "We must also focus on restoring the balance of magic. The dark mage's influence has left its mark on the land, and we need to heal the soil, purify the water, and encourage the growth of new plants."

Thorne's voice was filled with determination as he said, "And we need to ensure that the knowledge and wisdom of the past are preserved. We must protect the ancient tomes and artifacts that hold the secrets of our world."

Aeliana's presence was a calming force as she spoke. "We must also foster a sense of unity and hope among the people. They need to know that we are here for them, and that we will work together to rebuild Eldoria."

Thalindra nodded, her eyes filled with approval. "You have all spoken wisely. The path ahead will be difficult, but I have no doubt that you will rise to the challenge."

Borin's expression softened as he added, "You have proven yourselves to be true leaders. Your courage and determination will guide us as we rebuild our world."

Seraphina's voice was filled with warmth as she said, "We will support you in any way we can. Together, we will restore Eldoria and ensure that the darkness never returns."

The group felt a sense of relief and determination as they listened to the council's words. They knew the journey ahead would be long and difficult, but they were ready to face it together. Their bond had been tested, but it had not broken. They were stronger and more determined than ever.

As the council members extended an invitation for Elara and her friends to join the newly reformed council, the group exchanged thoughtful glances. The weight of this new responsibility was not lost on them, and each member grappled with their own doubts and fears about their ability to lead and protect Eldoria.

Elara took a deep breath, her heart pounding with anticipation. "We are honored by your invitation. We will do our best to serve Eldoria and guide it into a new era of peace and prosperity."

Kael nodded, his expression resolute. "We will protect our people and ensure their safety. We will rebuild our defenses and stand ready to face any future threats."

Lyra's eyes sparkled with determination. "We will support the villagers and help them heal. We will work together to rebuild our homes and our lives."

Eldrin's voice was filled with wisdom. "We will restore the balance of magic and heal the land. We will ensure that Eldoria thrives once more."

Thorne's expression was resolute. "We will preserve the knowledge and wisdom of the past. We will protect the ancient tomes and artifacts that hold the secrets of our world."

Aeliana's presence was a calming force, her eyes glowing with a soft, inner light. "We will foster unity and hope among the people. We will work together to ensure that Eldoria remains a place of light and hope."

Thalindra, Borin, and Seraphina nodded in approval, their expressions filled with pride and confidence. "You have our full support," Thalindra said. "Together, we will guide Eldoria into a new era of peace and prosperity."

As they left the sanctuary, the sun was beginning to set, casting a warm golden light over the landscape. Elara felt a sense of peace settle over her. They had faced countless challenges and overcome seemingly insurmountable obstacles. Their bond had been tested, but it had not broken. They were stronger and more determined than ever.

With renewed hope and determination, Elara and her friends continued their work, their hearts filled with the promise of a brighter future. Together, they would rebuild Eldoria and ensure that the darkness never returned. The journey ahead would be long and difficult, but they were ready to face it together, their bond unbreakable and their resolve unwavering.

The Promise of Tomorrow

The sun was setting over Eldenwood, casting a warm, golden light over the village. The air was filled with the scent of blooming flowers and the soft hum of magic, a testament to the hard work and determination of the villagers and their protectors. Elara, Kael, Lyra, Eldrin, Thorne, and Aeliana stood at the edge of the village, looking out over the restored homes and the land beyond.

"We've come a long way," Elara said, her voice filled with pride and a touch of sadness. "But there's still so much to do."

Kael nodded, his expression thoughtful. "We've faced countless challenges and made many sacrifices. But we've also forged bonds that will never be broken."

Lyra's eyes sparkled with determination. "And we've shown that no matter how dark things get, we can always find the light."

Eldrin raised his staff, the light at its tip glowing softly. "The balance of magic is being restored, and Eldoria is healing. But we must remain vigilant and continue to protect our world."

Thorne's voice was filled with resolve. "We will honor the memory of those we've lost by ensuring that their sacrifices were not in vain."

Aeliana's presence was a calming force, her eyes glowing with a soft, inner light. "Together, we will rebuild Eldoria and ensure that the darkness never returns."

As they stood together, reflecting on the journey they had taken and the challenges they had faced, Elara felt a sense of peace settle over her. They had come a long way since leaving Eldenwood, and the journey ahead would be filled with uncertainty. But she knew they were ready to face whatever challenges lay in their path.

"We've learned so much and grown stronger because of it," Elara said, her voice filled with determination. "We will continue to fight for Eldoria and protect our home."

Kael placed a reassuring hand on her shoulder. "And we'll do it together. No matter what comes our way, we'll face it as a team."

Lyra smiled, her eyes filled with hope. "We've proven that we can overcome anything as long as we stand together."

Eldrin's voice was filled with wisdom. "The future is uncertain, but we have the strength and the knowledge to shape it for the better."

Thorne's expression was resolute. "We'll ensure that Eldoria remains a place of light and hope for generations to come."

Aeliana's voice was like a gentle breeze. "And we will always remember the lessons we've learned and the bonds we've forged."

As the sun continued to set, casting a warm glow over the landscape, the group felt a renewed sense of purpose. They had faced countless dangers and overcome seemingly insurmountable obstacles. Their bond had been tested, but it had not broken. They were stronger and more determined than ever.

With renewed hope and determination, Elara and her friends set out on a new journey, ready to face whatever challenges lay ahead. Together, they would rebuild Eldoria and ensure that the darkness never returned. The journey ahead would be long and difficult, but they were ready to face it together, their bond unbreakable and their resolve unwavering.

As they walked away from Eldenwood, the village behind them a symbol of hope and renewal, Elara felt a sense of excitement and anticipation. The future was uncertain, but she knew they were ready to face it together. They had saved Eldoria from the darkness, and now they would work to ensure that it remained a place of light and hope for generations to come.

The final confrontation had tested their resolve, but they were stronger for it. And as they set off towards their next destination, their hearts were filled with the promise of a brighter future. Together, they would face whatever challenges lay ahead, their bond unbreakable and their resolve unwavering. The journey was far from over, but they were ready to face it together, their hearts filled with hope and determination.

www.ingramcontent.com/pod-product-compliance
Ingram Content Group UK Ltd.
Pitfield, Milton Keynes, MK11 3LW, UK
UKHW022313250125
454162UK00011B/45